'Ross. . .'

'Genevieve. . .'

Both spoke together, then stopped abruptly, staring at each other. Ross straightened, his face strangely bleak as he stared down at her.

'I know what you're going to say,' he said quietly, 'and I'm sorry, Genevieve. That was never planned. Blame it on the moonlight, the wine, or whatever, but rest assured that it won't happen again. I'm just as anxious as you to avoid any kind of personal entanglement. Our arrangement is purely business, nothing else, agreed?'

LEASE
ON LOVE

BY
JENNIFER TAYLOR

MILLS & BOON LIMITED
ETON HOUSE   18–24 PARADISE ROAD
RICHMOND   SURREY   TW9 1SR

*First published in Great Britain 1990
by Mills & Boon Limited*

© Jennifer Taylor 1990

*Australian copyright 1990
Philippine copyright 1990
This edition 1990*

ISBN 0 263 76683 7

*Set in 10½ on 12 pt Linotron Times
01-9005-47957
Typeset in Great Britain by Centracet, Cambridge
Made and printed in Great Britain*

CHAPTER ONE

IT WAS still raining.

Genevieve stared out of the window, searching the sky for any chink in its grey armour, but there wasn't even the smallest trace of blue.

With a sigh she turned away from the depressing sight and looked round the shop, her eyes lingering worriedly on the full tubs of colourful flowers. It was mid-May, almost the height of the florist's season, yet she'd hardly sold a thing for the past few weeks, thanks to the inclement weather. If it didn't break soon then she shuddered to think what would happen. She'd spent hours going over the books last night, but no matter how hard she tried to twist and turn the figures round it was obvious that she was running out of money fast. Another few days of this unceasing downpour and it would be all over bar the shouting, and Hearts & Flowers would be no more than just a pleasant memory.

More depressed than ever, she walked back to the work bench to finish off the last order she had on her books, a delicate arrangement of Dendrobium orchids and tiny rosebuds. With deft, skilful fingers she twisted lengths of pale pink ribbon into bows and pinned them to the edges of the white wicker basket before sitting back to view the effect.

It was beautiful, one of the best things she'd ever done, yet she knew there was no way she could charge the customer its full value. The man who had ordered it for his wife and new-born baby daughter had been poorly dressed, his face worried as he had hesitantly queried how much it would cost, and, in her usual impulsive way, Genevieve had almost halved the figure. The trouble was, kind hearts and business just didn't seem to mix—something her bank manager made a regular point of telling her!

The telephone rang and she quickly laid a tiny satin bow aside to answer it, praying it would be a customer, and one who could afford to pay.

'Hearts & Flowers. . . Good morning.'

'Hi, Gen, it's me. Vicky.'

'Oh, goody, just what I need, an order. . .I hope!' Genevieve said, grinning.

'Business that bad, then, is it?' Vicky asked with genuine sympathy.

'Worse. If this rain doesn't let up soon then your Mr Harper will need to find a new tenant as well as a new florist.'

'Oh, I hope not, Gen. Not after you've worked so hard on the shop this past year. Still, here's something to brighten your day—a nice big expensive order from my dear boss.'

'Thank heavens! I think the only thing that's kept the wolf from the door these past few months is the wolf himself! I don't know what I would have done without Ross Harper's frequent changes of lady-friend, and all the expensive bouquets he sends them. I only pray that none of them ever manages to catch him, or I may as well call it quits.'

Vicky snorted with laughter. 'Catch him! You must be joking. The woman isn't born who can catch

Ross Harper and get him to put a ring on her finger. Why, he makes Casanova look like a monk! Still, don't knock it if it's good for business.'

'Oh, I'm not knocking it, believe me. I'm truly grateful that he has the stamina for it all.' Genevieve chuckled softly as she jotted the order down on her pad.

Ross Harper, head of H.R. Holdings and owner of the shopping mall where she leased her shop, was a living legend in the town. Almost thirty now, handsome, rich and extremely successful, he was the most eligible man around, and also the most elusive. The first wistful sigh, the first veiled hint about matrimony reputedly sent him running for cover faster than a bear chasing honey! But still, as Vicky had said, it was good for business, and if he ever did decide to settle down and get married then Genevieve would be shedding tears along with a few hundred others. The only difference being that hers would be for all the lost revenue, not the lost man!

'Right, I've got all that. What happened to his last lady, by the way? What was her name now?' She flicked back through the order pad, smoothing a page open as she came to the place she wanted. 'Ah, yes, here it is. . .Rachel Anderson. Well, she didn't last long even by Ross Harper's standards. I only sent her flowers at the beginning of last week.'

'Seems our cool, blonde Miss Anderson wasn't quite so cool after all. She started to get a bit pushy, so Mr Harper's decided to move on.'

'Well, she's probably better off without him, isn't she?' Genevieve replied, pushing back a long silky

strand of pale brown hair which had come loose
from its ponytail.

'What! You mean you wouldn't give your eye
teeth for a date or two with him?' There was a touch
of disbelief in Vicky's voice under the light mockery,
and Genevieve smiled to herself. Vicky might make
a great show of mocking her boss's numerous, ever-
changing romances, but Genevieve had a sneaking
suspicion that she was as smitten by him as anyone.
The trouble was Vicky knew only too well that she
wouldn't stand a chance with him. To become one
of Ross Harper's women one had to be both beautiful and rich, and while Vicky might score quite well
on the first count she scored zero on the last. No,
poor Vicky had as much chance of being selected for
his attentions as Genevieve had herself!

'No. Sorry to disappoint you, my friend, but your
Mr Harper leaves me cold. I prefer a bit more to a
man than a handsome face and a full wallet.'

'Mmm. I'd like to hear you repeat that after he'd
turned on the charm a bit! Believe me, Gen, he can
be devastating at close quarters, absolutely lethal. I
defy any red-blooded female to withstand his
charm.'

'Well, I'll have to take your word for it, I suppose.
After all, Ross Harper and I hardly move in the
same exalted circles, so it's doubtful if I could prove
your theory one way or another.' The shop bell
tinkled and Genevieve glanced round, smiling at the
elderly man who had just come in. 'I've got to go
now, Vicky. I've got a customer and I don't want to
let him escape. I'll get that order out for you straight
after lunch, if that's OK.'

'Yes, fine. Thanks, Gen. Oh, and send the bill up as soon as you like. I'll make sure it gets paid right away.'

'Thanks.' Smiling at her friend's thoughtfulness, Genevieve hung up, then hurried through into the shop, her eyes widening in concern as she took in the soaked condition of the elderly man's hat and coat.

'Mr Roberts! What on earth are you doing out in this weather? You'll catch your death!'

Since she'd opened the shop just over a year ago Mr Roberts had been one of her most regular customers, coming in to the shop each week to buy flowers to put on his wife's grave. However, she would never have expected him to venture out in this downpour.

She hurried round the counter, her brown eyes worried as she saw the dark patches of rain soaked into his old beige mac, the trickles of water pouring from the battered brim of his trilby hat.

'Oh, I'll be fine, Miss Gray, really. I couldn't let Alice down, after all. It would take more than a drop of rain to make me do that.'

There was a slight raspiness to his voice, an unhealthy flush to his sunken cheeks, and Genevieve felt more worried than ever. From the look of him he was already running a temperature, and the very last thing he needed was to get another soaking walking up the hill to the cemetery. She made an instant decision, knowing her ever-noisy conscience wouldn't let her do otherwise.

'Look, Mr Roberts, you just tell me what you would like and I'll take the flowers for you. There's no point in you getting even wetter when I have to go that way to deliver an order.'

It was a lie, a little white one, but she knew he would refuse her offer if he thought he was putting her to any trouble.

'Are you sure? It's very kind of you. I don't like to take advantage, but I must confess I do feel a trifle shivery.' Even as he spoke a tremor shook his thin frame, and Genevieve cut in quickly before he could change his mind.

'Of course I'm sure. Now just tell me what you want, then get on home. What you need is a nice hot cup of tea and a couple of hours with your feet up in front of the fire.'

'You're a good girl,' he said, his lined face breaking into a gentle smile as he saw her obvious concern. 'A good, kind girl. You remind me of Alice, you know. She had that same instinctive kindness and compassion for people. Yes, you're very like her. I'm just glad that I've realised it before it's too late. It will solve something which has been bothering me for a while now.'

Was he feverish, rambling with the effects of the chill? For a few seconds Genevieve stared at him, real concern showing on her soft oval face, but he seemed quite lucid and normal as he selected a large bunch of tall flag irises. He paid for the flowers, his hands shaking slightly as he carefully counted out the money, then left, walking slowly along the street, his head bowed against the stinging onslaught of rain.

Genevieve watched him go, holding the flowers gently in her small slim hands, one finger rubbing softly over a perfect purple bloom. He really shouldn't be out in this dreadful weather, and if she'd had her van she would have insisted on driving him home, but unfortunately it was in the garage having yet another bit of surgery done on its poor tired engine. Cathy, her part-time assistant, had offered to collect it on her way in to work, but she wouldn't arrive for another hour yet. Far too long to keep the man waiting in the shop in wet clothing. She could only hope that he would follow her advice and go straight home.

Still bothered by the thought of the elderly man, Genevieve wrapped the flowers, adding a few sprays of lacy green fern to the bunch to give a delicate contrast to their stiff formality. She pulled on her raincoat and tied a scarf over her head before locking the shop and stepping out into the street. She shivered as the first cold drops slid down her cheeks, her generous mouth curving into a wry little smile. Rainwater was supposed to be good for the complexion, so it was said, so she should really look on the bright side and view this forthcoming soaking as a free beauty treatment. With the state her finances were in it was the only one she was likely to get!

What a day! First the almost total lack of sales, then the soaking, and now. . .this! This was just the icing on the whole miserable cake.

Genevieve stared down at the order pad, her brown eyes filled with worry as she tried to find some way to rectify the error, yet just what could she do? The flowers had been delivered now and

there was really no way she could arrive on Rachel
Anderon's doorstep, smile sweetly and explain that
they hadn't been intended for her but for some other
woman. . .another of Ross Harper's women, to be
precise.

'Oh, Gen, I really am sorry. I know I should have
double checked with you. I just never realised that
the order was for someone else.' Cathy's voice
wobbled as she tried to hold back the threatening
tears, and Genevieve patted her arm and murmured
soothingly, knowing she was more to blame than her
assistant. She should have checked the order before
she let Cathy take it out, as she usually did. It had
been sheer carelessness to tell her to get the address
off the pad, quite forgetting that she'd left it open at
the wrong page. No, if anyone was to blame for the
error then it was her.

The real problem now was to decide what to do
next. Should she send out another order to the
correct address, quietly forgetting about the first, or
should she ring Ross Harper and confess?

For a few nerve-racking minutes Genevieve nib-
bled on the end of her pencil while she debated the
merits of each solution, yet deep down she knew she
really didn't have a choice. There was no way she
could ignore what had happened, try and pretend
that everything was all just fine. What if Rachel
Anderson phoned Ross Harper to thank him, or
even worse, arrived on his doorstep to offer her
thanks in person? It could prove to be very embarrassing if he was entertaining the new woman in his
life, to say the least! While she had the feeling that
Ross Harper, with all his vast experience in the love

game, could probably handle any sort of situation, she wouldn't want to put anyone on the spot like that. No, she had no option but to phone him and explain what had gone on.

She looked up, forcing a smile to her lips as she saw the worry on Cathy's pale, strained face. 'It really wasn't your fault, Cathy,' she said gently. 'I should have checked that you had the right address before I let you deliver the order. Still, don't worry about it. I'm quite sure Mr Harper will understand when I explain. After all, it was a genuine mistake, so what can he do. . .shoot me?' She laughed, a slightly hollow note to the sound as she faced the fact that Ross Harper didn't need to go as far as holding a gun to her head to finish her off. He only had to withdraw his quite considerable business to start the first bell tolling!

'Anyhow, you run along now, Cathy. There's no point in you waiting round here any longer. I'll just give Mr Harper a ring, then I think I'll keep the shop open for another couple of hours. With the rain finally stopping I might just be able to grab some of the hospital visiting trade.'

She ushered Cathy out of the door, keeping the smile pinned to her lips as the older woman kept up her stream of apologies. When she had finally gone, Genevieve leant back against the cold glass panels and closed her eyes, desperately trying to work out what she should say in the forthcoming phone call. Obviously Ross Harper would be annoyed, but surely he would understand that it had been a genuine error? If he did decide to withdraw his custom, then. . . She closed her mind on that line of thought, knowing she could only cope with one horrible situation at a time.

On leaden legs she walked through to the tiny back office and dialled his number, feeling her heart start to hammer hard in her chest in sudden apprehension. The phone seemed to ring for ages before anyone answered, but it was only the night porter, who briskly informed her that the switchboard was closed for the night and to ring back in the morning.

Genevieve replaced the receiver and glanced at her watch, her eyes widening as she realised it was way past five-thirty. Somehow she hadn't realised it was already so late. She would have to leave the call till the morning, yet, somehow, the idea of the confession hanging over her head for the next twelve hours wasn't appealing. She would rather get it all over and done with now. She'd be a nervous wreck if she had to wait till the morning.

Pulling down the telephone directory, she flicked through the pages to find Ross Harper's home number, praying it wouldn't be unlisted. She ran a finger down the neat little column of names, feeling her hand tremble as she finally arrived at the one she wanted. She rubbed her damp hands down the side seams of her cord skirt before carefully dialling the unfamiliar string of digits.

The phone rang three times, Genevieve counted the peals, her heart hammering wildly in her throat. Then suddenly a deep voice answered and she drew in a shaky little breath and rushed into her speech.

'Mr Harper, this is Gen. . .' She got no further as the deep voice continued without a break.

'. . . speak after the tone.'

There was a sudden throbbing hum of sound and for a long second she stared dumbly at the receiver, wondering what on earth was going on, till she suddenly realised she was connected to an answering machine. Dropping the receiver back to its rest, she thought quickly, hastily rearranging what she'd intended to say, then dialled again.

'Mr Harper, this is Genevieve Gray of Hearts & Flowers, the florists, calling. I'm afraid there's been a mistake made in your delivery and the flowers you ordered today have been sent to Miss Rachel Anderson. I'm extremely sorry. I realise this could be—well, rather inconvenient for you, but it was a genuine error.' Had there been just the slightest touch of irony in her voice when she'd said that last sentence? For a split second, a mere heartbeat of silent time, she wondered about it, then with a shrug dismissed the idea. Even if there had been, there was little she could do about it now, with the messsage already taped. He would have to view it in whatever light he chose to.

As quickly as she could she said her goodbyes, then hung up and sat limply in the chair, feeling her whole body trembling with reaction. It had been one of the hardest things she'd ever had to do, making that apology and confession, but at least it was over. The trouble was she had the uncomfortable feeling that it wouldn't be the end of the affair by a long chalk!

Genevieve kept the shop open till seven o'clock, then, when trade started to slacken off, she began to close up. Though she was tired, it had been worth making the effort to stay open a while longer. There was more in the till than there'd been for most of the past week. Perhaps it would be worth doing it more often; a few hours' extra work was little price to pay for making the shop a viable concern.

She tidied up, brushing the floor and adding more water to the tubs of flowers, before walking wearily through to the back for her coat and bag. Automatically she glanced in the small square mirror, her hands lifting to push a few stray strands of hair back into place. Although her hair was very thick it was silkily fine, falling just past her shoulders as straight as rainwater. When she was working she always kept it pinned back off her face, hating the feel of it tumbling round her cheeks. For a brief moment she studied her reflection, taking stock of the neat, regular features, the pale olive tint of her skin which she had inherited from her French mother. Mid-brown eyes under strongly marked dark brows stared back at her, and she pulled a little face, laughing at her own unaccustomed vanity, before turning away to gather up her coat.

She shrugged the coat on, grimacing at the damp feel of the cloth against her skin, then picked up her bag and flicked off the lights. Even though it was supposed to be summer it was still rather dark in the shop, the leaden weight of the sky blocking out most of the light. Only a faint yellowish glow shining through the half-glassed door broke the rather eerie gloom. Everywhere was very still, very quiet, the whole mall deserted now that the other shopkeepers had locked up, and for some reason Genevieve started to feel a trifle nervous. There had been a couple of break-ins in the mall in the past few weeks,

and they had all been warned to be extra careful
when they left their premises, to make certain that
all the locks were securely fastened. Now, remembering the warnings, Genevieve wished she'd followed everyone else's example and left earlier. It
was unnerving to realise that she was the only person
left in the entire building.

Anxious to be gone, she hurried towards the door,
muttering crossly as her foot caught against a small
tub and knocked it over. She bent down to right it,
pushing the flowers back rather haphazardly, her
eyes locked on the small square of yellow light. For
a moment there, just as she had bent down, she'd
thought she'd seen something move, a tiny shadow
passing in front of the light. Was there someone
there?

The first tiny cold curl of fear spiralled through
her stomach and she straightened, her ears straining
against the silence for any hint of noise. Suddenly a
figure appeared, silhouetted against the door panel,
and she clamped a hand over her mouth to hold
back the scream that rose to her throat. Slowly,
cautiously, she inched her way back from the door,
feeling the blood pounding and rushing through her
head, making her feel dizzy. Who was it? What did
he want, standing outside her door? Nothing good,
she'd be bound!

As she watched, the door-handle started to turn
slowly, and with a sickening jolt of memory she
remembered that she had not bothered to drop the
catch before she started to close up for the night.
Whoever was out there was coming in, and there
was little she could do about it. . .or was there?

She spun round, snatching up the first thing which came to hand, a wooden mallet she used for crushing flower stems. Taking a firm grip on the handle, she hurried over and stood behind the door, holding the mallet aloft. So help her, whoever was sneaking in was going to be sorry, if she got even half a chance!

The door opened wider, something about the way it moved with such quiet stealthiness enforcing every single one of her fears, and Genevieve felt her breath catch tight in her throat. She closed her eyes, willing herself not to panic, to wait her chance and give the intruder exactly what he deserved. She might only have the one chance, and she had to take it.

A figure stepped into the shadowy darkness of the shop, hesitating just inside the doorway as though trying to get his bearings, and Genevieve gripped the mallet handle so hard that her fingers started to ache. Although she could see little apart from a dark outline there was no doubt in her mind that it was a man. The height, the sheer breadth of shoulder was just too pronounced for a woman. For a full minute he stood quite still and she had the sudden unnerving feeling that he had sensed she was there. A tiny moan of sheer terror murmured from her lips before she could stop it, and he swung round, his hand raising as though to strike her, and Genevieve knew she had to act now and act quickly.

She stepped forward, swinging the mallet at his head, hearing his muttered gasp as he tried to sidestep the blow, then a deeper one as it connected. As though in slow motion he slumped to the floor, the crack of bone hitting concrete sickeningly loud in the dark silence.

For one long, horror-filled moment Genevieve stared down at the shadowy figure, her legs trembling with a strange mixture of relief and terror. Then suddenly she came to her senses. She had to get help, phone for the police, the fire brigade, for whoever would come, before he came round.

She fled across the room, scattering tubs of flowers as she went, uncaring that her flying feet crushed the delicate blooms. Her one thought, her only one, was to summon assistance.

Flicking on the lights, she picked up the phone, shooting a quick nervous glance over her shoulder to check that he wasn't moving. Quickly, her eyes slid up the long length of his body before she dialled the first number, then slowly she hesitated as something tugged at her mind. A suit. . .the intruder was wearing a pin-striped suit. Surely that wasn't the customary attire for a burglar?

Finger resting in the niche of the telephone dial, she shot another glance at the man on the floor, her eyes taking rapid stock of the expensive suit, the snowy linen, the silk tie tossed limply over one broad shoulder, and felt the first tiny shiver of unease wriggle through her. Had she made some sort of dreadful mistake? Was this so-called intruder really a late customer?

Hands shaking, she dropped the receiver back into its cradle, then walked slowly back round the counter towards the still figure. He was lying partly on his side, the back of his dark head turned towards her, so that from this angle Genevieve couldn't get a glimpse of his face. Cautiously she edged closer, prepared to turn tail and run if he showed the smallest sign of movement, but he remained quite still.

She bent down, leaning forward so that she could get a better look at his face, and felt herself go cold in sudden horror. Standing up, she reeled back against the wall, fighting down the surge of panic, praying that she'd been mistaken, that the whole thing had just been some terrible sort of hallucination from start to finish—but of course it hadn't.

When she finally opened her eyes again everything was just the same: the same unnerving silence, the same potent smell of crushed flowers, the same still figure lying on the floor, a figure she recognised from all the numerous photographs she'd seen in the papers. . .Ross Harper. Had she killed him?

CHAPTER TWO

HE WASN'T dead. Sitting in the office drinking coffee
from a mug which for some reason kept missing her
lips by the tiniest fraction, Genevieve could hear
real evidence of the fact that Ross Harper was very
much alive.

For the past ten minutes, while the doctor she had
so hastily summoned had been ministering to him,
he had kept up a never-ending stream of curses
which was music to Genevieve's ears. At another
time she might have objected to the rough words,
but not now, not when she realised that she wouldn't
have to face a charge of manslaughter after all.
Assault, malicious wounding—oh, there were probably a dozen or so charges he would get her on, but
at least she'd been spared the trauma of that!

She glanced round, her eyes straying to the tall
figure slumped in the chair across the room, then
looked hastily away as he glared at her, his blue eyes
filled with loathing. Despite the purpling bruise on
his temple, the absolute pallor of his skin, he looked
ready to kill someone, and Genevieve didn't need to
be psychic to know that someone was her.

He had barely addressed a word to her since he
had regained consciousness, but then he'd not really
needed to bother with mere words. His hard-boned
face was filled with a barely suppressed fury which
proclaimed all too clearly what he thought of her,

and Genevieve wriggled uncomfortably in the hard, straight chair. It was obvious he was saving it all up until they were alone, so there would be no witnesses when he exacted his revenge, and suddenly the idea of prison didn't seem quite so unappealing. Prison might be the only place where she'd be safe from this man!

'Right then, Mr Harper, that should do it for now. I'll leave you some strong painkillers for that head-ache, but as far as I can tell you shouldn't suffer any lasting damage from the blow. It's just lucky that it didn't catch you further into the middle of your forehead; you wouldn't have got off quite so lightly then.'

The doctor shot a cold glance at Genevieve, and she had the grace to blush before staring down into the inky depths of her coffee.

What on earth had possessed her to overreact like that, to even consider using that heavy mallet in such a fashion? She was usually so calm, so com-pletely logical that such an action was right out of character.

She swirled the coffee round, grimacing as a large splodge of liquid spilled over on to her skirt, soaking darkly into the pale green corduroy. She put the cup down, linking her hands tightly together in her lap, feeling every single nerve singing out with tension. It felt as if she had a whole opera going on inside her, but was it any wonder, when in another few minutes the doctor would leave and she would be left alone with Ross Harper? The thought of what he would do and say was alarming, to say the least.

'Right, I'll be on my way, then. If the headache

persists tomorrow then I think it would be sensible if you checked with your own physician, but I'm sure the tablets will ease the worst of it. They're very strong, so you mustn't try and drive while you're taking them. I suggest that you get someone to take you home and then get some sleep. . . You, young lady, are very lucky that you aren't facing a charge of manslaughter,' the doctor said coldly, and Genevieve flinched back, her face paling even further as he continued. 'Are you quite sure that you don't wish to call the police and press charges, Mr Harper? I would be prepared to give a statement.'

Ross Harper stared quietly at him for one long timeless moment and Genevieve felt her stomach turn over as she considered the possibility of facing a court case. She held her breath, praying he would refuse the doctor's offer, then tried to call the prayer back as she heard the quiet menace in his voice when he answered.

'No, thank you, doctor, I don't feel there's any need for that. I would prefer to handle this myself without all the attendant publicity.' He glanced over at Genevieve, his long lips curled into an evil, mocking little smile, and she hastily bit back a soft moan of anguish.

The doctor left, closing the door quietly behind him, and Genevieve sat up straighter, fighting the urge to collapse into a grovelling little heap and beg for forgiveness.

'Well?' said Ross Harper softly, and for a second she wondered just how anyone could get so much meaning into a single word. She licked her dry lips and tried to get her brain to function, but it seemed to be paralysed with terror. All she could manage was a low mutter.

'I. . .I'm very sorry.'

'And that's it, is it? Don't you think you owe me some sort of explanation? I mean, do you always greet people with a blow to the head like that?'

'Of course not,' she said shortly, pricked into answering by his open sarcasm. 'Look, Mr Harper, I'm very sorry about what happened. It was just a dreadful mistake.'

'A mistake. . .another one? Seems to me you make an awful lot of mistakes, Miss Gray.'

So he'd got the message. Genevieve had known all along that he must have done—why else would he have come to the shop?—but she could really do without an inquest into that after what had just happened.

'All I can say is that I'm sorry, really and truly sorry about the flowers and, of course, this. Mind you, it was partly your own fault, of course.'

'My fault? I get hit over the head with this and it's my fault!' He tossed the wooden mallet on to the counter, and Genevieve jumped as it hit the marble. 'I may be dense, Miss Gray, or perhaps the blow to my head did more damage than I imagined, but please explain how any of this could be my fault.'

Cold sarcasm laced his voice, and Genevieve flushed, feeling her temper start to rise. Fair enough, she had been at fault for making the wrong delivery, but surely he could see that he was partly to blame for his injury, for creeping in on her that way.

She pushed the wisps of hair out of her eyes and faced him squarely, her brown eyes sparking. 'Of course it's partly your own fault! If you hadn't come pussyfooting in here like that, then I would never have hit you.'

'Pussyfooting! I don't go pussyfooting anywhere, for your information, lady.'

'No? Well, I'd say you were doing a fine imitation of it tonight. You nearly scared me witless, creeping in like that! Surely you've heard about the burglaries in the mall this past week, so is it any wonder that I was frightened and reacted like that?'

'And what exactly would any burglar find to steal in here? A few dozen roses, a couple of pieces of Oasis. . .oh, all very valuable, I'm quite sure!'

Genevieve's face flamed with angry colour as he shot a disparaging glance round the small, untidy room before turning back to her, one thick, dark brow raised in mocking enquiry.

She sat up straighter and glared back at him, wishing she could find something really cutting to say, but of course not one single thing came to mind.

'I see you've taken my point, Miss Gray. There's absolutely nothing of value here, nothing that anyone in his right mind would go to any trouble to steal. Nothing!' He roared the last word at her and Genevieve flinched back in her chair, feeling a spurt of satisfaction race through her as his face suddenly paled. He raised a hand to his forehead, rubbing it gingerly over the swelling bruise on his left temple, his blue eyes closed as though in pain.

When he spoke again his voice still held a thread of anger, but it was quieter. 'Look, Miss Gray, there's obviously no way we can continue this discussion at the moment. I suggest we leave it until the morning when you can come to my office.'

'Office? Why on earth do I have to come there? I mean, I've said I'm sorry, so what more can I do? I can't see how coming to your office will achieve anything.'

'Can't you? Well, I'm afraid I disagree. I think it will achieve plenty. I have no intention of letting this drop so easily.' He stood up, swaying slightly till he caught his balance, and Genevieve huddled deeper into her chair as she saw the harsh set to his strong features as he stared grimly down at her. 'Be at my office by ten, Miss Gray, no later. Not if you really value your business.'

He swung round, heading for the door, but Genevieve couldn't let him go like that without some sort of explanation of what he meant. She jumped to her feet and raced after him, catching hold of his arm with frantic fingers.

'Wait! What do you mean? What do you intend to do?'

'That, Miss Gray, is for me to know and you to find out, isn't it? Goodnight.'

Brushing her hand off his arm, he walked out of the door, and Genevieve stared after him, feeling her heart pounding in sudden apprenhension. Surely he didn't intend to put her out of business, did he, just because of one—no, two little mistakes?

With a heavy heart she switched off the lights and locked up, leaving the mess of crushed flowers and water to be cleaned up in the morning. She was just too tired to bother with it all then, too tired and too dispirited. If she'd interpreted Ross Harper's words correctly, then the shop mightn't be hers much longer, so what difference would any amount of tidying up make to anything?

Out in the street, she stood on the pavement for a few minutes, drinking in deep lungfuls of the cool damp air while she tried to regather her scattered senses, but it was difficult. It was barely eight o'clock, just an hour since she'd first started to lock up the shop, yet she felt as though a large part of her life had just rushed past her. An hour ago she'd been just Genevieve Gray, florist, quietly going about her business, yet now she had to come to terms with the fact that she had very nearly committed murder, and was facing possible eviction! What a difference a single hour could make!

Sighing to herself over the vagaries of fate, Genevieve glanced along the road—and froze as her eyes fell on the sleek sports car parked by the kerb, and on the tall figure lying slumped against its bonnet. Even from this distance, with the grey-blue bloom of twilight distorting everything, it was hard not to recognise Ross Harper, and she felt her stomach lurch in sudden fear. What was wrong with him? Why was he half lying across the car like that? He'd seemed well enough when he left the shop, a trifle unsteady perhaps, but strong enough to walk, and defintely strong enough to start planning some sort of reprisal. So what had happened now?

With a marked reluctance she turned towards him, hurrying across the few yards of pavement to stand next to him.

'Are you all right?' she asked quietly, her eyes running over the stark pallor of his face in concern. Against the white skin the bruise stood out lividly,

the purpling flesh swollen and angry-looking, and
Genevieve felt a sudden wave of remorse rise up and
swamp her. How could she have ever done that to
him? She would never have believed herself capable
of such violence.

'No, I'm not all right,' he said grimly, his blue
eyes flicking open to stare at her with open dislike in
their depths. 'I feel bloody awful, if you really want
to know.'

He swayed slightly, his big body sagging against
the side of the car, and instinctively Genevieve
stepped forward and put her arm round him. It was
obvious he was on the verge of collapsing and she
knew there was no way she could walk away and
leave him like this. She was responsible for his
condition, and whether she liked it or not, she had
to make certain that he got home safely.

Looping his arm over her slim shoulders, she said
firmly, 'Look, you're in no fit state to drive tonight.
The doctor already warned you against trying. I'll
have to take you home. Can you walk a few yards to
my van?'

'I'm not going anywhere with you! Don't you
think you've done enough damage for one day? I'd
be a fool to entrust myself to you.' With a vicious
tug he attempted to pull his arm free, groaning
deeply as the sudden movement jarred his head.
Genevieve kept a firm grip of his arm, refusing to let
him go, though nothing would have given her greater
pleasure.

'Frankly, Mr Harper, I don't think you have a lot
of choice in the matter, do you? Unless you can
think of someone you'd like me to call to come and

fetch you, it's a question of either spending the night out here on the pavement or letting me drive you home. If it gives you any comfort then remember that I don't relish the prospect any more than you. Now come along.'

With a firmness that belied the nerves which were leapfrogging round her stomach, Genevieve half led, half dragged him down the street, propping him up against the side of the old van as his long legs started to buckle. She leant against him, using her slight weight to hold him upright while she scrabbled in her bag for her keys, then carefully and laboriously helped him inside.

He was tall, a good six inches or more than her own five feet five, his body big and heavily muscled, so that by the time she had accomplished this feat she was exhausted. She closed the van door and leant against it for a few moments while she caught her breath, then hurried round and slid behind the wheel.

'Has anyone ever told you that you're a bully, Miss Gray?' he asked, his deep voice mocking yet softer than she'd heard it before.

She slipped the key into the ignition, then shot a look at him, her brown eyes wary. 'Frequently. Now close your eyes and rest. I don't know if I've got enough strength left to carry you when we get there.'

He chuckled softly, then groaned before resting his head cautiously against the hard cushion. Genevieve eased the van into gear and pulled away from the kerb, fighting against the sudden dizzying tightness in her chest. With the anger gone from his face, and his eyes holding little more than a teasing

mockery, Ross Harper was devastating, and she was
reeling from the effect.

She clung hold of the steering wheel, forcing
herself to concentrate as she drove the van carefully
through the city streets. She had to remember that
Ross Harper was nothing to her, nothing but the
owner of her shop, the man who was now threatening to take her livelihood away from her, yet,
somehow, it seemed strangely hard to remember
that simple little fact.

Genevieve slowed the van to a crawl, steering it
gingerly along the rutted path, wincing as the
exhaust scraped against a mound of stones. She
switched her headlights on, flicking them to main
beam as she tried to select the most even route down
the twisting driveway. Next to her Ross Harper held
his head in his hands, his voice sharp as he said
crossly, 'For heaven's sake, can't you slow down,
woman! You're not competing at Le Mans, you
know!'

Well, so much for their brief truce, and all those
silly little daydreams which had accompanied her on
the drive. Now they were back to exactly where
they'd started! Genevieve glared at him, then hastily
turned back to the road as the van lurched sideways
over a particularly evil hillock of loose gravel.

'Don't blame me. If you didn't choose to live in
such a godforsaken spot then I wouldn't have to go
risking life and limb, not to mention my poor
exhaust, getting here,' she snapped back nastily.

'Godforsaken? I'll have you know the house is set
in one of the most beautiful spots you could ever

hope to find round here,' he shot back at her. 'The only reason the drive is in such a state is that I'm having some renovation work done, and the builders' lorries keep cutting it up when they race down it. They were probably taught at the same driving school as you, from the look of it!'

Obviously pleased at getting the last word, he braced himself against the seat and closed his eyes again, and Genevieve fought down the sudden urge to aim the van at a huge billowing rut and press down hard on the accelerator. Only the thought of the damage she might do to the old van and the subsequent repair bill stopped her from doing it.

She eased her foot off the pedal and slowed down to a meagre five miles an hour, rueing the impulse which had made her offer to drive him home. She should have left him where he was, out in the street, rather than make this awful journey and suffer his insults. Quite frankly, if she'd had any idea that it was going to take over an hour to get to his home then she would never have made the offer. It would be nigh on midnight before she got back home to her own bed at this rate.

A dark outline came into view, and she breathed a sigh of relief as she realised they were nearly at the house. She rounded the last bend and glided to a halt, her eyes widening as she got her first glimpse of Ross Harper's house.

Stunned, she climbed silently out of the van, staring up at the crazily angular lines of its roof, the spiralling points of the twin towers, and gulped. It was dreadful! The whole thing looked like something out of a horror movie. All it needed was a few fluttering bats, a couple of bloodcurdling screams, and it would be perfect. What on earth had possessed him to buy such a place?

'Well, what do you think?' Ross Harper struggled out of the van and leant limply against its side, his eyes holding an unmistakable gleam of pride as he studied the wretched building. Genevieve swallowed hard, desperately trying to find something nice to say, but it was a losing battle. What could any sane and rational person find to say that was nice about this. . .this monstrosity?

She clamped her lips together and murmured something unintelligible.

'What? What did you say?' He turned sharply to her, a vague suspicion on his face that her remark had been less than complimentary, then he closed his eyes, swearing softly as the sudden movement made him dizzy.

'Come along, let's get you inside.' Genevieve saw her chance to evade the issue and grabbed it quickly, not wanting to be drawn into any further arguments with him. All she wanted was to get him settled and leave as fast as she possible could. This damned house, on top of everything that had happened, was enough to give her nightmares!

She took him firmly by the arm and helped him up a shallow flight of steps to the huge front door which looked as if it could have withstood a charge by any amount of cavalry. He leaned heavily on her for a second while he felt in his pocket for the key, then slowly unlocked the door and motioned her to enter.

With dragging steps Genevieve walked inside,

waiting till he flicked on the lights before venturing
further, remembering all too vividly all the horror
films she'd ever seen. She looked round, not quite
able to stifle the gasp of dismay that sprang to her
lips as she saw the piles of rubble, the stacks of
broken wood leaning drunkenly in every corner. The
whole place looked as though a bomb had hit it;
surely he couldn't really live here, could he?

'Mmm, looks a bit of a mess, doesn't it? Still, wait
till you see it in a couple of months' time, then it will
really open your eyes. Once the carving on that
banister has been restored, and the wall panels have
been stripped and varnished. . .well. . .'

He glanced round with obvious pride, picturing
the finished article. For a moment Genevieve studied him, feeling surprised that a man like Ross
Harper should go to so much trouble to restore the
building. She would have expected him to prefer
somewhere slicker, smarter, the proverbial high-tech
bachelor pad, rather than this old and ugly house. It
showed her a different side to him, a side far
removed from the glittering lifestyle portrayed in the
frequent newspaper articles about him. Somehow it
worried her that he no longer slotted neatly into the
category she'd placed him in.

'I can see that you don't have a lot of imagination,
Miss Gray,' he said coldly, his blue eyes flicking
sharply back to her. 'Obviously you can't picture
how the place will look when it's finished.'

He sounded annoyed, and hastily Genevieve
brought her thoughts back to the present problem.
There was no way she wanted to antagonise him

further, to promote another argument. Her livelihood could depend on it! She fixed a politely bland
expression on her face, a cool, smooth smile on her
full lips, suddenly anxious to get away. She'd done
quite enough damage for one night to last her a
whole lifetime.

'I'm afraid I was daydreaming, Mr Harper. I'm
sure the house will be beautiful when it's all completed. Now, is there anything I can get you—a
drink, a cup of tea? Or do you have a housekeeper
to look after you?' She glanced round as though
expecting a suitably black-clad vision to materialise
along the hall.

'Not as yet, though when I do actually move in I
suppose I shall have to hire one. The house is rather
large for me to manage on my own.'

'When you mo. . .don't you live here now?'
Genevieve's smooth brow wrinkled a trifle as she
glanced round again before turning back to him.

'Of course not. The house won't be ready for
months yet. Good heavens, look at it! It's hardly
habitable, now is it?' He laughed as though she'd
just made some sort of joke, but Genevieve couldn't
find anything amusing about it. She rounded on him,
her face set, her body stiffening with sudden temper.

'Then why on earth did you get me to bring you
here? Where do you live if you don't live here?' Her
voice rose a full octave as she asked the question
and she saw him wince before putting a soothing
hand to his throbbing temples.

'Do you really need to shout like that? I have a
flat in town, about ten minutes' drive from the mall.
That's where you phoned tonight.'

'But I don't understand. What's going on?' A cold shiver raced up her spine as she stared up at him, cursing herself for not having paid more attention on the drive over. If she'd only stopped to think about it she would have realised that the address he'd given her was different from that in the phone book. The trouble was, she'd been so bowled over by the dazzling smile, the touch of charm, that she'd never even thought about it.

She ran her eyes over him from top to toe as he stood calmly in front of her, and shivered. In the pale eerie glow from the cobweb-laced chandelier he looked somehow different, taller, darker, a touch more menacing, and cautiously she began to edge her way towards the door, wondering if she'd made the biggest mistake of her life. Had he changed his mind about getting his revenge on her through her business? Had he now decided on a more personal course of action? After all, the house was lonely, way off the beaten track; no one would hear if he. . .

'Where are you going?'

The low-voiced question stopped her dead. Genevieve glanced down at her feet as though surprised to find them moving. She swallowed hard, gripping the strap of her bag between her shaking fingers.

'I. . .well, I think it would be better if I left, don't you? It's getting late, and I'm sure you're dying to get to bed, so I think I'll say goodnight. I'll see you in your office tomorrow.' An hour ago the thought of going to the office had terrified her, now the thought of the alternative was even worse!

'And leave me here alone. . .without even the benefit of a telephone?'

'What do you mean?' Brown eyes filled with uncertainty, she stared at him, seeing the tiny smile that flickered across his lips with a sudden trickle of unease. What was he up to? Why did she have the feeling that he was playing some sort of elaborate game with her, a game she didn't know the rules of?

The thought stiffened her spine, added a touch of strength to her quivering voice. 'Look, Mr Harper, just what is going on? Why did you get me to bring you here?'

'Where else could I go? Back to the flat to await Rachel and all her fulsome thanks for the flowers you wrongly sent her? No, I don't think I'm up to fending off her unwelcome attentions tonight, thanks to you, Miss Gray.' He touched a long finger to his head and Genevieve glanced down at the dusty toes of her black shoes, not quite able to meet his eyes.

'I. . .well, I think I can understand that, Mr Harper,' she said quietly, 'but it still doesn't explain what's going on now.'

'No?' He lifted his hand to ease his tie loose, flicking open the top buttons of his shirt to expose a few inches of strong, tanned throat, and for some reason Genevieve found her eyes drawn to the tantalising glimpse of bare flesh.

'It's really quite simple, Miss Gray. I shall have to spend the night here now, and I was hoping that you would agree to stay with me.'

His voice was low, deep, the soft tones hypnotic almost, and it took Genevieve a few moments to register what he'd just said. She gasped, her hand racing to her mouth to stifle the sound, knowing how much it betrayed her sudden agitation.

'What?' she cried. 'What did you just say?'

He chuckled softly, the sound rippling through the silence. 'Oh, I think you heard me correctly the first time.'

'Yes, I did! Spend the night here. . .with you? Why, the blow must have caused more damage than anyone anticipated! I think you should call the doctor out again, Mr Harper. Get him to check you over once more!' Anger ripped through her voice, added a flush of colour to her cheekbones as she flounced towards the door. Grasping the handle, she started to pull it open when he spoke again, so quietly she had to strain to hear him.

'With what? There's no telephone here, Miss Gray. No help close at hand. No one to call to if I need assistance. Can you really turn your back on me and walk out of that door? Will your conscience really let you do that?'

Maybe if he'd threatened her, cajoled or even ordered her, then she could have done it, could have walked out of the door without a second thought or backward glance, but not now. Not now he'd stirred her noisy conscience to life.

Letting her hand slide from the lock, she turned back, knowing she was beaten.

CHAPTER THREE

DAMN her conscience. She hoped it felt as stiff and cold as she did!

With a soft little groan Genevieve pulled herself upright, putting a hand to her back to ease the aching muscles. She swung her feet down off the footstool and stood up, staggering slightly as her numbed legs threatened to buckle under the weight of her body.

Across the room, snugly bundled under the folds of an old satin quilt, Ross Harper was sleeping as peacefully as a baby, and she stifled the urge to make some sort of loud and violent noise to waken him. All night long, as she'd moved her cold cramped body from one lumpy spot to another in the old armchair, Ross Harper had been snoring gently, the soft, regular rhythm more irritating than anything Genevieve had ever experienced. It just wasn't fair that he should be able to sleep like that while she'd been tossing and turning. Why should she have been the only one to suffer?

With a tiny sigh of annoyance she crept from the room, closing the door quietly behind her. She glanced at her watch, her eyes widening as she realised it was barely six o'clock. It felt far later than that, as though she'd just spent a major part of her life in that room listening to that damned man snoring, not just a mere eight hours. She'd gone into that room a fit and agile woman; now she felt as though she'd just aged twenty years. Would she ever be able to walk again without hearing her joints snapping and cracking? Would she ever be able to turn her head without feeling her neck creaking? She doubted it.

Thoroughly out of sorts with the world, she made her way slowly along the hall to the kitchen, or at least to the room which Ross Harper had assured her would be the kitchen in a few months' time. Now, standing in the doorway, staring round at the piles of debris, the bare walls and crumbling plaster, Genevieve wondered if he was being a trifle over-optimistic. It would take years to turn this place into a kitchen, surely?

She crossed the room, wincing slightly as her stockinged feet crunched over tiny mounds of dust and plaster, and other objects she didn't have the stomach or nerve to investigate too closely. She filled the kettle and plugged it in, before rinsing two chipped mugs under the tap that flowed into a stained stone sink. There was no tea-towel to dry the mugs, so she contented herself with shaking them briskly, then rubbed them quickly up the sides of her jumper. Beggars couldn't be choosers, or so the saying went, yet she doubted if any beggar could be as ill-equipped as Ross Harper seemed to be in this dreadful house. He must have been mad to suggest spending the night here, mad or completely desperate. Surely Rachel Anderson couldn't be as pushy and determined as he'd implied, could she?

'So, there you are. I wondered what you were up to.'

Genevieve jumped, her eyes shooting to the tall
figure that stood in the doorway, feeling the colour
flood to her cheeks in a sudden tide. She glanced
down, staring at the mugs held tightly in her hands,
while she tried to stem the sudden rhythm of her
heartbeat.

'What's the matter? Did I frighten you?'

He came further into the room, a faintly puzzled
expression in his eyes as he studied her heightened
colour, and Genevieve grabbed hold of the excuse
he'd just given her and hung on to it. She couldn't
afford to admit that her confusion stemmed from
something other than mere surprise. It would be too
dangerous to do that, too foolish to admit, even to
herself, that with his black hair rumpled and the
faint shadow of stubble darkening his jawline he
looked so devastating that for a moment he had
quite taken her breath away. She had to remember
that this was Ross Harper, playboy, womaniser, a
man she had always viewed with scorn before. She
couldn't allow his obvious physical attractions to
influence her.

'I didn't hear you come in,' she answered shortly,
turning away to set the mugs down with a sharp little
clatter. She spooned coffee into the mugs, cursing
softly as the tiny granules scattered across the table.
The kettle was almost boiling, so she switched it off
and made the drink, breathing in the familiar aroma
with a feeling of relief. It was good to have such a
mundane task to do, to cling hold of reality in such
a way. Ross Harper and his lifestyle were way out of
her league.

'Here.' She held one of the mugs out to him, pleased to see her hand was steady again.

'Thank you.'

He took the mug and sipped the drink with obvious appreciation, his eyes still locked to her face, and Genevieve hunted round for something to say to break the faint tension that hung between them.

'How do you feel today? Has your headache gone?' Picking up her own drink, she sipped the burning liquid while she studied the livid bruise marring the smooth tanned skin of his temple.

'Not too bad, I suppose, considering I hardly got any sleep last night. Has anyone ever told you that you snore, Miss Gray?'

'Me? What do you mean I snore? Oh, that's rich, really rich, coming from you, Ross Harper! I'll have you know *I* never got a wink of sleep because of *your* snoring. It sounded as if you were sawing logs all night, so don't try blaming me for your supposed tiredness. You were well away!'

Hectic colour stained her cheeks a brilliant carmine as she glared at him, feeling her temper rise even higher as he chuckled softly.

'What's so funny?' she demanded curtly.

'You. Are you always so short-tempered, ready to bite a person's head off at the least provocation?'

'I am *not* short-tempered! In fact, I would go as far as to say that I'm positively renowned for my even temper!' Genevieve almost roared the denial at him, fighting back the urge to toss the cooling dregs of her coffee into his mocking face. 'It's just you. . .you seem to have some sort of a horrible effect on me, that's all.'

'Do I indeed? Mmm, I shall have to remember that for the future. It could be useful.'

There was an undisguised innuendo in his deep dark voice, and Genevieve glared coldly at him before turning away to stare out of the window while she mouthed a few million nasty comments. She wouldn't say anything more, wouldn't retaliate, wouldn't come down to his level. But he made her so furious, so utterly livid! She couldn't ever remember feeling like this about anyone before. She was usually so level-tempered, so cool, calm and proverbially collected, so why did this one man have such a disastrous effect on her?

'I'm sorry, I didn't mean to tease you like that,' he said softly. 'It's just that you react so beautifully that it's irresistible.'

His sudden apology surprised her. She looked over her shoulder, her brown eyes searching his face, but he seemed quite sincere. It would be both churlish and childish not to accept it at face value.

'Well, I suppose I'm partly to blame. I'm tired and edgy because of what's happened, so maybe I have been overreacting a trifle. Look, Mr Harper, about last night, when I hit you and the flowers and everything, I really am so. . .'

'I know. . .sorry. You've told me before, several times, and believe me, I accept your apologies, if only to stop you from repeating them.'

There was a wry twist to his mouth, a gleam of humour in his deep blue eyes, and Genevieve turned quickly away, feeling her heart pounding like a wild thing. She drew in a deep breath, then sipped the last of the cold coffee, desperately trying to get her wayward feelings under control. Oh, he had an effect on her all right, and it wasn't just on her temper, that was the pity of it! Anger she could handle, but this strange breathless feeling that gripped her each time he smiled at her was something way beyond her control.

'Beautiful, isn't it?'

'What?' She hadn't heard him moving closer, hadn't realised that he was now standing just behind her. She flicked a swift glance at him, feeling her blood-pressure rocket another few notches as he smiled at her, his face gentler than she'd seen it so far.

'The view, of course. Look, just over there, to your right.' He set his cup down and gripped hold of her shoulders, his big hands gentle as he turned her to face the direction he wanted. 'Now look, beyond that dip in the land. Can you see how the sun just touches the trees and skims back off the lake? Looks like fairyland at this time of the day.'

Almost absently he rubbed his hands up and down the length of her arms, and Genevieve held herself rigid, forcing herself to concentrate on the view and not on the tantalising pressure. She stared out of the window, watching the rosy-gold light gild the tops of the trees and bounce fire off the glittering water, and sighed. He was right, it was beautiful, more beautiful than anything she'd seen in a long time. She knew she would remember this moment for years to come.

'Well?' he asked softly. Genevieve shivered delicately as his warm breath whispered over the curve of her cheek. He was so close that she could feel the heat from his tall body against her backbone, could feel the lean hardness of his muscled frame. At that moment she would have given anything to stay exactly where she was, watching the beauty of the sunrise, feeling the closeness of the man, but she couldn't. It was far too dangerous to do that, to let her guard slip and forget just who he was.

She stepped away from him, smiling faintly, her eyes not quite meeting his. There was no way she wanted him to know what a deep impression those few minutes had made on her.

'Yes, it is very beautiful. I think I can understand why you want to live here now. It would be worth putting up with all this just to see that view each morning.'

'Oh, the house will be equally beautiful when I've finished with it. All it needs is a bit of insight and imagination and you could see that for yourself.'

It was obvious from his tone that he didn't think she possessed such qualities, and Genevieve felt herself bristle at the slight. She had always considered herself sensitive, able to see beauty in almost anything. However, she doubted if anyone apart from this poor deluded man could view this ugly house as a thing of beauty!

She drew herself up to her full height, her face cold as she stared back at him.

'Well, I suppose time will tell, Mr Harper, but frankly I think you're wasting both your time and your money on this. . .this monstrosity. Now, if you're ready, shall we make our way back to town? I'm sure you'll be quite safe now. I doubt if Miss Anderson will have spent the night lying in wait on your doorstep!'

She swept out of the room, head held regally high, muttering crossly as she ruined the effect by stumbling over a loose floorboard. She shot a quelling glance over her shoulder, but for some reason he wasn't laughing as she'd expected. Instead he was watching her with an expression in his eyes that made her blood turn to sudden freezing ice as she interpreted its meaning.

She was going to pay for that last remark, and from the look of it pay dearly! Lord help her, what had she done?

The journey back was accomplished in a heavy brooding silence that strained Genevieve's already stretched nerves even further. Ross Harper sat in the passenger seat staring out of the window, his face totally impassive. With the bruise standing out in a brilliant rainbow hue of colours on his temple and his suit rumpled and his hair dishevelled, he should have looked anything but intimidating, but he did. So intimidating that Genevieve felt her knees turn to water.

Why had she goaded him like that, allowed her foolish, hasty tongue to run away with her? He'd seemed so reasonable before, far calmer than the previous evening; ready, almost, to forgive if not forget her misdemeanours. Now, after that last crack about Rachel Anderson, she doubted if he'd be ready to forgive her anything!

From the look of it he was plotting something, and she didn't need to be Sherlock Holmes to guess that that 'sómething' had to do with her. She had the sudden nasty feeling that she was now teetering on the edge of a precipice, and that very soon Ross Harper was going to make the final move to push her over. She could only pray that the fall wouldn't be too hard or too far.

'Can you drop me at my flat first? I need to get changed before I pick up the car. I have an appointment at nine.'

His voice was cool, politely level, yet Genevieve felt her heart lurch, then race wildly as she heard it. She glanced towards him, wondering why she had the sudden inexplicable feeling that the request held some deeper significance than a mere desire to get ready for the coming meeting.

Had there been just the slightest inflection in those deep tones then, just the faintest nuance? Biting her lip, she re-ran the words fast through her brain, but she couldn't pinpoint what it was that bothered her. Was she getting paranoid, seeing double meanings and hidden dangers where there were none? After all, surely it was only logical that he would want to change out of his crumpled clothing before starting work.

Somewhat reassured by the sense of the thought, Genevieve murmured her agreement and drove steadily on into the city. Traffic was light at that early hour of the morning and she made good time. Following Ross Harper's precise directions, she had no difficulty in locating the exclusive block of flats where he lived, and was soon turning into the driveway, feeling a surge of relief wash through her that the ordeal was nearly over. Another few minutes, another few polite apologies and, she hoped, acceptances, then she would be able to relegate Ross Harper and the whole miserable business to the very back of her mind. All things considered, she'd come out of it fairly well unscathed.

She cut the engine and turned towards him, a warm little smile of relief curving her lips, a smile which first wavered, then disappeared completely when he spoke.

'Thanks. Why don't you come up and have some coffee while you wait? I won't be long.'

Swinging the door open, he stepped out of the van before Genevieve could gather her wits about her fast enough to ask him what he meant. Wait? Why on earth should she wait?

She flung her own door open and hurried after him, catching hold of his arm to halt his progress.

'What are you talking about? Why should I wait?' Her brow wrinkled into a tight little furrow as she stared up at him, searching his face for any clue to the puzzling statement, but it was impossible to read anything in his expression.

'Naturally, I assumed you would wait while I changed and then drive me into town to collect my car. After all, it is your fault that it's been left there all night. I only hope nothing has happened to it.'

There was a coldness in his voice that struck a chill down Genevieve's backbone. Her hand slid from his arm as he stepped forward to pull the door open, standing aside for her to precede him with a mocking courtesy that made her teeth snap sharply together.

In sullen silence she led the way across the foyer towards the lift, quelling the urge to stamp her feet with vexation on the hard marble floor. If she had only realised that he was going to do this then she would never have agreed to drive him to the flat. Only the thought of what he might do stopped her from marching straight out of the building. No, in this instance it seemed that Ross Harper was indeed the piper, and she would have to dance to his tune. But as soon as she had delivered him to his car then that was it. He wouldn't see her again for dust! What had Vicky said about him yesterday. . .that he was charming, and that she doubted any red-blooded woman could resist that charm? Well, Genevieve was about to prove her wrong. As far as she was concerned, Ross Harper was about as charming as a double-headed rattlesnake!

The lift whisked them up to the penthouse level of the building, its metal doors sliding smoothly open on to a small square hallway. Ross Harper stepped out of the lift first, feeling in his pocket for the key to unlock the single mahogany door that led off from it.

Genevieve followed him slowly into the flat and along a narrow passage, pausing in the doorway of the huge living-room. For a few quiet minutes she stared round, taking rapid stock of the acres of creamy-pale carpet, the plush black velvet sofas, the huge array of expensive and sophisticated audio-visual equipment banked along one whole wall, and grinned.

The whole room was a mirror image of where she had expected him to live, in a designer-decorated, hi-tech apartment. . .the traditional bachelor pad. It was far more in keeping with his reputation as a playboy than that old and ugly house would ever be, and she felt herself relax a trifle as he slid once more back into the neat little niche she had allotted him.

Here, in this flat, he was Ross Harper again, a man who neatly fitted the image she had always held of him, and suddenly Genevieve felt more sure of herself than she'd done for ages. She turned to him, her face composed as she said calmly, 'Where's the kitchen? I'll put coffee on while you get ready.'

For a moment Rose Harper stared back at her, his eyes narrowed as though trying to assess what had caused the sudden change in her attitude, but Genevieve maintained her aura of calm, refusing to be ruffled. That other Ross Harper, the man who had held her by the shoulders and made her watch the sunrise with him, could disturb her all right, but not this one. She had no time for men like this, who took their pleasure with scant regard for others.

Something of her feelings must have shown on her face, because his eyes suddenly hardened and his voice was curt almost to the point of rudeness.

'Over there. That door on the left.'

Genevieve nodded, then strode confidently towards the door he indicated, feeling him watching her every step of the way. She shot a quick glance over her shoulder just in time to see him disappear through another door, and chuckled softly. If Ross Harper thought he could get the upper hand this time then he could think again! Nothing, absolutely

nothing, was going to shake her composure now. It
was rock-solid.

Humming softly to herself, Genevieve briskly
opened cupboard doors at random till she found the
things she wanted. She filled the coffee-maker with
water, then spooned ground coffee into the filter and
plugged it in, waiting patiently while it dripped a
stream of fragrant dark liquid into the glass jug.
Opening another cupboard, she found cups and
saucers and arranged them neatly on the small glass
breakfast table before hurrying back across the
living-room, her feet sinking into the soft carpet.
She paused just outside the door where Ross Harper
had disappeared.

'Coffee's ready.'

'Oh, fine. Thanks. I won't be long. Tell you what,
why don't you make us something to eat? I don't
know about you, but I'm famished. There's eggs and
bacon in the fridge. Can you cook?'

Of all the nerve! Just who did he think she was,
the maid or something! Hands on hips, Genevieve
prepared to tell him in no uncertain terms what he
could do with his eggs and bacon when he appeared
in the doorway, and she felt the words freeze on her
part-open lips. In stunned silence her eyes swept
over him from head to toe, and she felt colour surge
to her cheeks.

Dressed in tight-fitting dark trousers and little
else, with his tanned chest bare and his black hair
still damp from the shower, he was enough to rob
the words from any girl's lips, and quite frankly,
Genevieve was no exception. For one long, appreciative moment she allowed her eyes to linger on

him, then looked up, feeling her face flame even more as she caught the glimpse of mockery in his blue eyes.

It was obvious that he'd experienced this sort of reaction before, and she turned away, hating herself for giving him that much satisfaction. Had it only been coincidence, a purely innocent act that had made him appear like that, or had he planned it, right from the beginning, just to throw her off balance? She didn't know, but frankly she wasn't prepared to give him the benefit of even the slenderest doubt!

'Is there something wrong, Miss Gray? You look. . .well, flustered.' The mockery was open now, and Genevieve drew in a deep breath, forcing herself to meet those wicked, laughing blue eyes with an outward show of calm. It was the only way she could hope to cling on to her self-esteem.

'No, of course there's nothing wrong. I'll make a start on that breakfast, shall I?'

She hurried back to the kitchen, hearing the soft sound of his laughter trailing after her as he watched her go. Closing the kitchen door, she leant against the sink for a moment, feeling the coldness of its smooth steel top biting into her hot damp fingers. She closed her eyes, desperately trying to find that lovely veneer of calm and composure which she'd had before, but it seemed to have disappeared completely now.

If it weren't for the fact that she knew it would give that damnable man such pleasure, she would have walked right out of the flat that very moment and worried about the consequences of her actions

later. But she had to stay, had to show him exactly
what she was made of!

She set to work on the breakfast, working quickly
so that by the time Ross Harper appeared in the
kitchen doorway she already had the bacon sizzling
and the toast browning. She shot a quick glance at
him, feeling her traitorous pulse leaping at the sight
of him standing there, a pale blue silk shirt empha-
sising the darkness of his hair and the golden colour
of his skin.

'Mmm, that smells good!'

Crossing the room, he pulled out a chair and sat
down at the table, watching Genevieve while she
broke an egg into the frying pan. Aware of the
scrutiny, she felt her hands start to tremble slightly
so that she hit the shell far harder than she intended
and watched with annoyance as the yolk broke,
oozing deep yellow across the hot pan.

'Sorry. Am I making you nervous?'

His voice was low, slightly smug, and Genevieve
shot him a cold look, wishing she had a tub of
arsenic handy to add to this breakfast. She steeled
herself and broke a second egg into the sizzling fat,
shooting him a quick look of triumph as it landed
safely, its yolk perfect. Quickly she splashed the egg
with fat till the yolk filmed over, then slid it on to a
plate along with several rashers of crisp bacon,
setting it down in front of him with a sharp little
clatter.

'That looks lovely, thank you.' He picked up his
knife and fork and cut into the bacon, his eyes lifting
to where she stood hovering uncertainly next to him.

'Aren't you having anything? Surely you must be starving after last night?'

Genevieve turned away, wiping her hands on the dishcloth lying on the counter, forcing her jangling nerves to calmness. The worst was over now, only a matter of another few minutes, half an hour at the most, then she and this man could part for ever. She could afford to let herself relax a little and join him at the table for a cup of coffee. There was no danger in that.

She picked up the jug and poured two cups of the dark, fragrant coffee while she spoke. 'I never eat anything cooked for breakfast. I'll just have coffee and maybe a slice of toast.'

'Pity. You don't know what you're missing—this is delicious. You wouldn't be interested in a house-keeping job, by any chance, would you?'

His voice was gently teasing and Genevieve felt herself relax even further, enough, in fact, to turn and smile at him.

'No, thank you. I'm quite happy with what I do now.'

'Of course—your shop. How is business?'

He returned his attention to his plate, mercifully missing the faint unease that crossed her face as she tried to work out how to answer that question. She didn't want to actually lie and give too glowing an account of the shop's progress but, equally, she didn't want him to get any doubts as to its viability as a business concern. After all, he was her landlord, and she didn't want him to think she couldn't meet her obligations as a tenant. The lease was due for renewal in a few months' time; she couldn't afford to do or say anything that might endanger it.

Perched uncomfortably on the horns of the dilemma, she took her time sitting down at the table and spreading butter on a piece of toast while she gave herself a chance to review her options. She looked up, aware that Ross Harper was watching her closely, a faint hint of something in the depths of his eyes that immediately alarmed her.

'I. . .well, yes, the shop is doing quite well, I suppose. I mean, it could do better, but of course that probably applies to any business, doesn't it?'

She bit a tiny corner from the triangle of toast and chewed it slowly, waiting to hear what he would reply. Had her hesitation in answering done the very thing she'd wanted to avoid and alerted him to the fact that she was having problems? She watched closely as he set his knife and fork aside, then picked up his cup, sipping the hot coffee gingerly. He looked at her over the rim of the cup, his face impassive, yet she had the strangest feeling that his quick brain was rapidly weighing up what she'd said. Ross Harper hadn't got where he was today, head of a huge multi-national concern, without some sort of inbuilt business sense and gut feeling for when things might be wrong. He must have realised almost immediately that her answer had been evasive, to say the least, and she silently cursed herself for the slip.

'You don't sound too certain, Miss Gray. Is there something wrong at the shop? Aren't you doing enough trade to cover your overheads?'

'Yes, of course I am,' she answered, just a shade

too quickly. 'Admittedly business has been slow this past week or so, because of the weather, but I usually manage to make a living.'

There was a slight defensiveness in her voice, and Ross Harper smiled before lowering his cup back to its saucer.

'Why do I get the feeling that you're not telling me the full story? Are you covering up something. . .the fact that the shop is barely doing enough trade to stay open? Still, no matter. I'm sure we'll get a full picture when your lease comes up for renewal. We usually ask to see your books and cash-flow projections, just to safeguard our interests. Our accountants pride themselves on being able to suss out any suspect deals.'

A chill shivered its way up Genevieve's backbone, but she forced herself not to show just how much his words worried her. Would her books stand up to a close and expert scrutiny, confirm the fact that the shop would soon be the thriving concern she hoped it would be? Only time would tell, time and all Ross Harper's numerous accountants. Her livelihood, her dreams of owning the best, most successful florist's shop in the city lay in their hands. She could only pray that they would treat both gently.

'More coffee?' Ross Harper stood up, holding his hand out for her cup, and Genevieve watched with troubled eyes while he poured the drink. He set it down in front of her, smiling faintly as he slid his long legs under the table.

'Don't look so worried! I'm sure everything will be fine. Business is quite often slow in the first two years. It takes time to build up a reputation. Mind you, if you make too many mistakes as you did yesterday, then you could find yourself in trouble fast. One thing a customer needs to know is that his order will be despatched safely and accurately.'

'I know,' she said miserably, staring down into the depths of the coffee. 'I really am sorry about it. I know you're probably tired of hearing it, and that it doesn't change anything, but it really was an accident. I just hope it won't stop you from using Hearts & Flowers again for your orders. I could go round to Miss Anderson's house and explain, if you want me to. I could probably find some way of not letting her know that the flowers were really intended for another of your. . .your friends.'

'Oh, I don't think that will be necessary. No, I'm sure the situation will resolve itself very shortly.'

'Resolve itself. . .? What on earth do you mean?' Startled, she stared at him, her brown eyes dark with confusion. 'I. . .'

The doorbell rang, the soft rolling sound of its chimes cutting off her words. Ross Harper stood up, a faint, enigmatic twist to his lips as he said softly, 'You'll see.'

He strode out of the kitchen and Genevieve stared after him, the delicate cup cradled in her hands. She took a sip, then set it back on its saucer with a tiny clatter, wondering why she had the sudden, horrible feeling that something was about to happen. From the direction of the hall came the sound of voices, moving closer, and she looked towards the open doorway, wondering who it was at this early hour.

'But, darling, where were you? I must have phoned a dozen times last night and called round to see if I could catch you in. And how did you get that dreadful bruise on your. . .'

The woman's voice tailed off abruptly as she walked into the kitchen and caught sight of Genevieve sitting at the table. She stopped dead, her face paling as she glanced from her to the man lounging carelessly in the doorway.

'Ross?'

'I don't think you two have met, have you?' he asked softly, watching the little tableau with a strangely flat expression on his face. 'Genevieve, I'd like you to meet Rachel Anderson. Rachel, Genevieve Gray. Why don't you join us for some coffee, Rachel? I'm sure there's still some left from breakfast. . .just. We were both so ravenous after last night that we've finished everything else off.' He moved into the room to pick up the glass jug, swirling the scant inch of liquid round in a dark whirlpool that held Genevieve's stunned, hypnotised eyes. 'Yes, just enough for another cup.'

There was a curious silence in the room when he stopped speaking, as though time had suddenly ground to a halt. Then, as Genevieve finally managed to drag her gaze away from the jug, she saw a look of cold comprehension cross the tall blonde's face.

'You bastard, Ross Harper!' she said furiously, then swung on her heel and stormed out of the room, slamming the front door behind her with a force that made the whole place shake.

For one long, disbelieving minute Genevieve stared up at him, scarcely able to comprehend what she had just witnessed. She stood up, her whole body shaking with anger as she rounded on him.

'You did that deliberately, didn't you? Brought me here, knowing that she would call round, let her think that we'd spent the night together!'

He shrugged, his big shoulders moving briefly, nonchalantly under their light silk covering. 'Of course. And after all, it wasn't a lie. We did spend the night together.'

'Not in the way she meant, we didn't! How could you do that? How could you be so cruel?'

'Sometimes you have to be cruel to be kind, Miss Gray. Look, I've been trying to shake Rachel off for a week or so now, but I'm afraid she's been deliberately deaf and blind to any of my subtler hints. After you'd sent her those flowers, I knew things would become impossible. This seemed like the best way of getting through to her, to make her realise, once and for all, that our affair is over.' His voice was harsh, without the tiniest thread of compassion, and Genevieve felt her anger turn to disgust. She pushed past him, knowing she couldn't bear to stay in the flat a second longer.

'Where are you going?' He caught her arm, swinging her round to face him, but she wrenched herself free, her brown eyes filled with an icy contempt that brought a rim of colour to his cheekbones when he saw it.

'Home,' she snapped.

'And what about our agreement? I thought you were going to drive me into town to collect my car.'

'That was before I realised exactly what sort of a rat you are. I don't take vermin in my van with me!'

'You'll regret that,' he said softly, his face and voice filled with an anger which at any other time would have sent Genevieve into a paroxysm of terror. But not now. Not now she'd realised exactly what sort of a man she was dealing with.

She stood up straighter, her whole bearing one of regal dignity as she faced him squarely. 'Do what you like, Ross Harper,' she said quietly. 'Do whatever your nasty twisted mind can come up with because, quite frankly, I'd rather face that then stay here a second longer. The thought of being in the same room as you makes me feel sick!'

She swung round, walking out of the kitchen and across the living-room, not even flinching at the sound of china shattering. As far as she was concerned that was it, the end of the whole affair. From now on Ross Harper no longer existed.

CHAPTER FOUR

FOR someone who didn't exist, Ross Harper managed to claim a disproportionate share of Genevieve's waking and sleeping thoughts. As the days crept past, crawled into a week, she found herself going back time and again over what had happened that disastrous night and even more disastrous morning. She might wish that she had heard the end of the whole affair, yet deep down some sort of sixth sense warned her that Ross Harper would never let it rest at that. The look on his face as she'd swept out of the flat that morning had spoken volumes!

Not that she regretted her actions, her refusal to condone his heartless treatment of Rachel Anderson, but she would have been a fool not to wonder just what he would do to pay her back. She didn't know, couldn't even guess what form the reprisals might take, but she *knew* he would think up something unpleasant, and the nagging worry about what was to come pervaded her life, lingering like a dark foul shadow, tainting everything she did, day after day.

Towards the end of the second week after the incident, Genevieve was sitting in the back of the shop working on a wedding order. The wedding, planned for the following day, was to be the local social event of the year, and she was more than a little pleased that she'd been asked to do the flowers.

Besides the bride's bouquet, the posies for the bridesmaids and all the buttonholes, she had been asked to do displays to decorate the church. It was a sizeable order, the biggest one she'd been given since opening the shop, and she knew she should make a healthy profit from it. By staying open late most nights during the past couple of weeks she had managed to break even last month, but the business was still teetering dangerously on the edge of bankruptcy. This little bonus should take it one step further away from the edge.

Humming softly to herself, she set to work on a delicate corsage for the bride's mother, carefully binding the fragile stems of freesias on to their wire frame. The telephone rang, the strident noise unnaturally loud in the silence, and with a tiny gasp of alarm she dropped the flowers, muttering crossly as several of them fell to the floor. Wiping her damp hands down the sides of her jeans, she picked up the receiver and wedged it against her shoulder as she stooped to gather them up.

'Hearts & Flowers. . . Good afternoon. Can I help you?'

'Miss Genevieve Gray, please.'

The voice was cool, politely distant, yet for some strange reason Genevieve felt her heart leap with a sudden cold surge of apprehension. Slowly, carefully she straightened, laying the flowers gently down on the long worktop before gripping hold of its grainy wooden surface.

'This is Genevieve Gray speaking.' Her voice sounded strained, tense, and she coughed softly to ease the tight knot from her dry throat.

'I have a call for you, Miss Gray. Please hold the line.'

There was a series of soft clicks and hums, then a man's voice came over the line, the unfamiliar tones clipped and precise.

'Miss Gray?'

'Speaking.'

'Good, good. My name is Swan, of Swan, Swan and Fitton, Solicitors. I was wondering if. . .'

Genevieve didn't hear any more as her mind went blank with a numbing horror. Solicitors! Why was any firm of solicitors calling her. . .unless it had something to do wtih that wretched man Harper? Oh, she'd been expecting something all right, but never that he would go to a solicitor! The very thought of what he must be planning made her go suddenly icy cold all over, and she shivered, gripping hold of the counter with hands that had started to tremble.

'Miss Gray. . .are you still there?'

There was a touch of irritation in the precise voice now, and Genevieve took a slow deep breath and forced herself to answer. She had to stay calm, find a way out of this if there was one. There was no way she could afford to panic.

'Ye-yes, I'm still here, Mr Swan.'

'Oh, good, good. For a minute there I thought we'd been cut off. Now, Miss Gray, as I was saying, it's a. . .well, a rather delicate matter which I don't feel it would be appropriate to discuss over the telephone. Is it possible that you could arrange to come into my office either today or tomorrow at the latest? I hate to rush you, but the matter is rather urgent.'

'Well, I. . .' Genevieve hunted round for a few long seconds for some sort of an excuse to refuse the request, her mind racing a shaky path through a dozen possibilities from a visit to a sick aunt to an imminent trip to Outer Mongolia, but with a sinking heart she realised she couldn't use any one of them. It wouldn't take any great detective skills to discover her whereabouts at the shop, so just what was the point in refusing? After all, what difference would a few days' or even a few weeks' delay make to the outcome? No, if Ross Harper had engaged this solicitor to deal with her and her misdemeanours then frankly there was no excuse apart from death that would deter him! Anyway, surely nothing could be as bad as this dreadful waiting had been.

She licked her dry lips and spoke slowly, feeling her stomach wobbling with a sudden attack of nerves.

'I can come tomorrow, Mr Swan. Around eleven would be best if that's convenient.'

'Fine, fine. That suits me perfectly. Thank you, Miss Gray. I shall look forward to meeting you then. Our offices are in the High Street, next door to the Bank.'

It was obvious that the man was eager to end their conversation, but Genevieve couldn't let him go without making some attempt to find out something more.

'Mr Swan! Just a moment. Can't you tell me what it's all about? It all seems rather mysterious.'

'I really don't think it would be advisable to

discuss it over the telephone, Miss Gray. There are other parties involved.'

'These other parties,' she said sharply. 'Could one of them be Ross Harper, by any chance?'

There was a split second's silence and Genevieve felt her hopes slide even further as she realised she'd guessed correctly that Ross Harper was involved. The man's faint reluctance to answer the question was proof in itself.

'Don't bother answering, Mr Swan,' she said shortly. 'I can understand that you don't wish to compromise yourself in any way. I shall see you tomorrow.'

She replaced the receiver slowly and sat quite still, staring blankly into space. She'd known all along that Ross Harper had been plotting something, yet somehow she'd never imagined that he would draw a third party into his plans. Obviously he didn't intend to soil his hands when he could get someone else to do the dirty work for him. Now how on earth was she ever going to last the next twenty-four hours till she found out what he intended?

The sun was shining, one of those warm soft days which come so rarely and should be treasured, yet Genevieve could find little pleasure in the touch of the sun on her bare arms. She made her way slowly along the High Street, past the Bank, and stopped, her eyes lingering on the black-painted door, its gleaming brass nameplate bearing the legend, 'Swan, Swan and Fitton, Solicitors'.

She glanced round, idly winnowing the silky sweep of pale toffee hair away from her hot neck, trying to

summon up enough courage to go in. Across the
road the church clock struck the hour, and automatically she glanced at the plain gold watch strapped to
her wrist to check the time. Eleven o'clock, on the
dot. There was no way she could afford to linger out
on the pavement any longer. No matter how hard
her heart was thumping and her pulse racing, she
had to go in and meet the fate which was awaiting
her on the other side of that neat dark door. It was
the hardest thing she had ever done.

Taking a deep breath, Genevieve strode briskly
up the shallow flight of scrubbed stone steps and
pushed open the door, hesitating for a moment while
her eyes adjusted to the cool dimness in the hallway
after the bright hot glare outside in the street. A
series of closed doors led off from the hall and she
walked slowly past them, stopping at one marked
'Reception' before stepping inside.

The girl sitting typing at a desk glanced up and
smiled faintly at her.

'May I help you?'

'Yes. I have an appointment with Mr Swan at
eleven. The name is Gray, Genevieve Gray.'

The girl ran a long red-lacquered nail down the
appointment diary and nodded. 'Yes, here it is.
Please come with me, Miss Gray. I'll take you up.'

She slid out from behind the desk and led the way
out of the room and up a steep flight of stairs,
scarcely giving Genevieve time to catch her breath
before she ushered her into a huge, bright, airy
room. For a few seconds Genevieve stood just inside
the doorway, blinking rapidly as rainbow flashes of
sunlight blurred her vision, then slowly, as her eyes

adjusted to the brightness of the light, she realised that there was not just one man in the room but two. . .an elderly man in a stiff black suit, and Ross Harper!

For a long minute she stood and glared at him, her brown eyes sparking, her whole body filled with a rage she'd never experienced before in her life. Then Mr Swan spoke, his clipped tones breaking the tense silence.

'Miss Gray. It's good of you to come at such short notice.'

Genevieve glanced at him, her expression bleak as a winter's landscape, seeing him for what he was. . .Ross Harper's hired man.

'Did I really have a choice?'

'Ahh. . .mmm. . .I. . . Won't you sit down, Miss Gray.' Obviously nonplussed by her open hostility, though Genevieve couldn't for the life of her see why he should be when he knew the reason why she was there, he pulled a chair into the centre of the room, placing it just a few feet away from Ross Harper. Genevieve sat down, quite deliberately settling herself at an angle so that her back was presented to him. She might be forced to be in the same room as the wretched man, but nothing on this earth would induce her to look at him again!

She stared coldly straight ahead, her eyes fixed on Mr Swan, who had sat down behind the desk and was now lining up pens and blotter with a painstaking precision that set her teeth on edge. When everything was finally arranged to his liking, he clasped his thin hands together and looked up, a faint curiosity in his pale eyes as he studied the grim set to her features.

'I believe you already know Mr Harper, Miss Gray,' he said politely, his glance skimming to Ross Harper before shooting back again as though he'd just seen something that alarmed him.

For a moment Genevieve was tempted to glance sideways, but she curbed the urge, refusing to give Ross Harper that much satisfaction. She might be worried, terrified even, but there was no way she was going to let him know that. She nodded briefly at the solicitor, her own hands clasped tightly round the strap of her pale beige leather bag.

'Good, good. That at least saves us from having to go through all the preliminaries. We can get down to business straight away.' The solicitor drew a thick folded wad of paper out of a large buff envelope and spread it out on the blotter, his gnarled hands smoothing the creases out till Genevieve felt she would scream with frustration. Why didn't he just get on with it? Tell her exactly what it was that Ross Harper wanted? Why did he have to keep up this charade of politeness and civility?

She bit her lip to stop the hot words from escaping and stared straight ahead, forcing down the wave of sheer irrational panic welling inside her. After all, what could Ross Harper really do? Surely his options were limited to either suing her for the blow on the head, or trying to find some way to foreclose on her lease. Either way he would find he had a fight on his hands. There was no way she was going to give in to him and his bullying tactics without a struggle!

'Ah, yes, here it is. The very passage I wanted.'

Mr Swan slid his glasses off his nose and looked up at Genevieve. 'Now, Miss Gray, I'm sure you must have heard about the sad death of Mr George Roberts. It was reported in the local papers, of course.'

He sat and watched her, obviously expecting her to confirm that she had heard about it, but for a full minute she just stared blankly at him. What was he talking about? Who was George Roberts, and what did he have to do with any of this?

She shook her head, her body stiffening as Ross Harper spoke for the first time, the deep tones sending a shiver of instant recognition up her backbone.

'Mr Roberts was my grandfather, Miss Gray. He died last week and, as Mr Swan said, it was widely reported in the local paper, as was his funeral. Perhaps you were too busy to bother about it.'

There was ice in the deep voice, a note almost of scorn, and unwillingly Genevieve shot him a startled glance, wondering what he was implying. Why should she know anything about his grandfather? She had never met anyone by the name of. . .

In a sudden blinding flash she realised who he meant, and her hand flew to her lips to stem the gasp of sorrow.

'Ah, I see you do remember him, then. . .at last,' Ross Harper said coldly, angry colour edging his hard cheekbones. 'Took you long enough, didn't it? Though I suppose it can be difficult remembering one elderly man from all the others you've. . ."befriended"!'

There was a barrel of double meanings in his

voice, but for a moment Genevieve was too shocked by the news of Mr Roberts' death to take him up on any one of them. Her eyes misted with tears as she remembered his weekly vists to the shop, their brief conversations, the way he had always treated her with a touching old-fashioned courtesy. That Ross Harper was his grandson was news to her. It was hard to imagine gentle Mr Roberts being the grandfather of this man. He'd obviously not inherited any of Mr Roberts' characteristics. In fact, Attila the Hun seemed a more suitable relative for him!

'Oh, spare us all the false grief, please, Miss Gray. Believe me, it cuts no ice. If you'd had any real feelings whatsoever for my grandfather then you would have done what dozens of others did last week and attended his funeral.'

The biting contempt was just what Genevieve needed to restore her composure. She swung round in the chair and glared at Ross Harper, her face still pale but set.

'For your information, I didn't know anything at all about Mr Roberts' death. I was so busy last week that I never had time to read any of the papers, local or otherwise.'

'I find that hard to believe, Miss Gray.'

'I don't give a damn what you believe,' she snapped back. 'Your opinions don't mean anything to me. From what I've seen of you, Ross Harper, you're hardly qualified to make moral judgements about anyone!'

For several seconds they sat and glared at each other like two prizefighters in opposing corners. Then suddenly Mr Swan cleared his throat, his thin lined face filled with concern and discomfort as he drew their attention back to him.

'Please, please, Miss Gray. . .Mr Harper. I know this is a very painful time for all of us, but I'm sure it won't help if you start arguing. I'm quite certain that would be the very last thing George Roberts would have wanted.'

He was right, of course. Genevieve had the grace to blush as she acknowledged the fact. She looked away from Ross Harper's angry face and stared down at her hands, wondering why he had this uncanny ability to make her forget her manners and behave so abominably. For a moment she considered apologising to the solicitor, but changed her mind the instant Ross Harper spoke. That man was completely insufferable!

'You're wasting your time, Swan, trying to reason with her. She's the most unreasonable female I've ever had the misfortune to come across!'

Well, that was it; the final straw which not only broke the camel's back but buried it in the sand along with all her good intentions! Genevieve stood up, her back rigid as she glared from one man to the other. 'I came here in good faith today, Mr Swan, at your request, but if you think that I'm going to stay here and be insulted by this. . .this. . .this apology for a man then you can think again. I have better ways of passing my time, believe me!'

Ross Harper crossed one long leg over the other and leant back in his chair as he stared up at her, obviously not one bit put out by her anger.

'Sit down,' he said quietly, his blue eyes like chips

of glacial ice as they met her burning brown ones. 'Sit down and stop making such a ridiculous scene.'

'Why should I?' Genevieve demanded hotly, clutching hold of her bag with trembling fingers.

'Why? Oh, I can think of a very good reason, Miss Gray. Half a million pounds' worth of good reasons, in fact.' There was a biting, icy contempt in his deep voice and on his face, but Genevieve scarcely registered it as she looked back at him, her brow wrinkling in confusion.

'What do you mean?' she demanded. 'What sort of riddles are you talking now?'

'Riddles. . .I wouldn't call a bequest for half a million pounds' worth of shares in H.R. Holdings a riddle, would you?'

'Bequest? What bequest?'

'My, my, you do act a good part, don't you, my dear Miss Gray?' he said mockingly. 'Why, anyone watching would almost believe that you knew nothing about my grandfather's plans to leave you half his shares in the company. How did you manage to persuade him to do that, I wonder? What little tricks did you employ to influence a lonely old man?'

It was blatantly obvious from his tone what he meant, and Genevieve felt the temper she'd held in check boil up and froth over. Reaching out, she caught him a stinging slap across his hard cheek, watching with a comforting sense of satisfaction as the mark of her fingers turned a nice clear scarlet against his tan.

'Why, you little. . .!' He leapt to his feet, his face contorted with rage, his big body quivering with temper as he towered over her, and Genevieve

realised that this time she'd overstepped the mark
by yards, not inches. This time there was no way she
would get away with taking a swipe at him. There
was murder in his face, and she didn't have to look
far to find the intended victim.

She spun round and hurried towards the door,
wrenching it open with enough force to set it bounc-
ing on its hinges. Behind her Mr Swan had risen to
his feet and was watching the scene with a mounting
horror on his face, scarcely able to believe that such
a thing could happen in his office.

'Miss Gray, wait, please, I implore you!' he called,
his voice quivering with distress.

Genevieve paused in the doorway, shooting a
brief glance over her shoulder, then took to her
heels as Ross Harper took a step towards her. No
matter who begged her, she wasn't going to risk
spending another minute in the room with that
madman. From the look on his face it would take a
whole army to protect her from him, not just one
elderly gentleman!

She fled along the corridor and down the stairs,
all too aware of the sound of someone hurrying after
her. Desperate to escape, she increased her pace,
her feet flying down the steep narrow treads. Suddenly the heel of one high sandal caught in a fold in
the carpet and with a tiny shrill scream of alarm she
pitched forward, bumping and banging her way
painfully down the rest of the stairs before hitting
her head on the heavy carved newel-post at the
bottom. Rainbows of brilliant colours swam in front
of her eyes, followed by bright flashes like a shower
of a thousand stars, then slowly everything started

to go dark. As though from a great distance she could hear someone calling her name and just for a moment she struggled to force her heavy eyelids open, groaning at the effort it cost her.

A dark figure was bending over her, the face blurred, the features distorted, yet Genevieve knew who it was. With a tiny moan of fear and anguish she let her lids drop closed, cutting off the threatening presence of Ross Harper.

Lord, how her head ached! Inching herself up against the lumpy cushions, Genevieve tried to hold back the moan as pain sliced through her head, making her feel giddy and sick. She lay still again, breathing deeply, trying to get the pain to drop to a bearable level, but it seemed to take an incredibly long time to die down. It felt as if the top of her head was going to blow off and she clamped her fingers in her hair to stem the eruption.

'Here, try this. It should help.'

The voice was unmistakable, and Genevieve's eyes shot open in alarm, her whole body freezing in sudden terror. Ross Harper was sitting on a low stool next to the couch, his jacket off, his shirtsleeves rolled up, his dark face impassive.

'Here.'

For a long minute Genevieve stared dumbly at the folded square of damp linen in his strong hand, then slowly she took it from him and held it against her temple. She closed her eyes again and lay back, letting the numbing coldness of the wet cloth seep into the ache while she desperately tried to think her way out of yet another awkward situation. The problem was she was just too weak to find any sort of a solution.

'How do you feel now? That's quite a bruise you've got there, almost as good as the one I had after you hit me with that mallet.'

Of course he would have to bring that up again, wouldn't he, even in her present condition? Genevieve glared coldly at him, her lips clamped thinly together, but he seemed not at all put out by her refusal to answer. He reached out and ran a long finger down the side of her face, smoothing the loose curling tendrils of soft hair away, and she shivered. She edged away, freeing herself from the strangely unsettling touch of his flesh against hers, biting her lip as the room started to spin. It felt as though she was trapped on some sort of fairground whirligig, spinning faster and faster, and with a tiny moan of distress she put the cloth to her lips as a sudden wave of nausea gripped her.

'Come on, don't try to fight it.' A strong arm lifted her upwards, holding her firmly till the miserable retching spasm abated. Genevieve opened her eyes, her face flushed with embarrassment that she should make a show of herself in front of Ross Harper of all people.

'I'm sorry,' she muttered, feeling the beet-red colour sweep up under the stark pallor.

'What for? For being sick, or for being so frightened of me that you risked injury by racing down those stairs? Seems to me that it's I who owe you an apology. Now just rest while I get rid of this, and see if I can rustle up a cup of hot sweet tea for you.'

'I hate sweet tea,' she said automatically, her eyes following as he stood up, bowl in hand.

'Well, like it or not, sweet tea is what you need and sweet tea is what you're going to get.'

If she'd only felt a bit stronger then she would have argued the point on principle, but Genevieve knew that her head was just too delicate for yet another confrontation. With a mutinous set to her lips she leant back and closed her eyes, hearing the soft sound of his mocking laughter as he quietly left the room. For the moment, at least, he had the upper hand, but when she felt better then he would soon find her far less amenable to his orders. Still, in all honesty she had to admit that he had been unaccustomedly kind to her just now. The big question was—why? What was he after? She had a feeling that kindness was not one of Ross Harper's usual attributes.

For several minutes she tried to work out what exactly was going on in Ross Harper's handsome head, but finally she had to give it up as a bad job. Even without this dreadful headache she would be hard put to it to come up with an answer, so right at the moment she didn't have a chance. No, if Ross Harper was plotting and planning something then undoubtedly she would find out what it was soon enough. For the moment she would be better advised to concentrate on the real problem at hand, namely the bequest. Was it true? Had Mr Roberts really left her all those shares in H.R. Holdings, and if so, why? Why should he leave them to her, a virtual stranger?

The door opened before Genevieve was even

halfway to guessing the answer to the puzzle, and she glanced round nervously, expecting to see Ross Harper in the doorway. However, this time it was the secretary she'd met earlier, balancing a delicate china cup and saucer in her hand.

'Mr Harper said you would like some tea, Miss Gray.'

'Thank you.' Genevieve took the cup from her, shuddering as she took the first sip of the hot liquid. He obviously hadn't been joking about the sugar; there must have been several large spoonfuls in the drink! She forced herself to drink it all, then handed the empty cup back to the girl, somewhat surprised to find that she did feel a little better. Her head was still aching, the bruise on her temple still very tender, but the weakness seemed to be easing from her limbs. Though she hated to admit it, that disgusting tea seemed to have done the trick.

Cautiously she swung her legs over the side of the couch, jumping slightly as the secretary said sharply, 'Oh, no, Miss Gray! Mr Harper was most insistent that you shouldn't try to get up yet. Please stay there. I'll just go and call him.'

It was obvious from her tone that Ross Harper's instructions held the weight of the Almighty, so Genevieve did as she was requested rather than cause the girl any distress. She sat back on the lumpy seat and stared round the small drab room, wondering what was going to happen next. So far, nothing had gone as she'd expected, so there was no way she could even begin to guess what was to follow. All she knew, with a deep-seated certainty, was that she had no intention of accepting the bequest. It had

been a lovely gesture and she would always be glad
that Mr Roberts had valued their friendship enough
to make it, but her conscience would never let her
accept something that belonged to another. H.R.
Holdings was Ross Harper's company and he should
retain full control of it. It was only fair.

'So you're feeling better, are you?'

Ross Harper stood in the doorway, watching her,
and Genevieve spun sharply round, startled that she
hadn't heard him, then groaned as her head started
to spin again. She swallowed hard, fighting against
the threatening attack of nausea, taking a few seconds before she tried to answer.

'I don't feel so bad now. I hate to admit it, but
that disgusting tea seems to have done the trick.
You were quite right about it.'

'I'm right about a lot of things, Genevieve Gray,
but the problem is that you can't seem to see it.'

'Listen, if you're referring to what you said earlier,
about me influencing your grandfather, then you're
wrong. Mr Roberts and I only ever met in the shop
when he came in to buy flowers. We would talk for
a few minutes, maybe half an hour sometimes, but
that was it. He was a gentleman and always treated
me as a gentleman would. There was never anything. . .well, anything. . .' She stopped, unable to
find just the right word to describe what he'd implied
before. That anyone could imagine she would do
such a thing as try to influence a lonely old man like
that was horrible.

Her huge soft eyes filled with tears at the very
thought and she looked away, hating to let him see
any sign of weakness. Ross Harper had already

proclaimed himself the enemy; it wouldn't do to give him a weapon to use against her.

'Maybe, maybe not. I suppose time will tell, one way or another. Look, perhaps I was out of order before in what I said to you—I realise that now. It's just that the bequest came as a complete shock. I'd always expected Grandfather to leave all the shares to me. Naturally, when I found out that he had left half of them to you, a stranger, I was furious. I need those shares to retain full control of the company, so it's left me with a whole cartload of problems, but somehow we shall have to work them out.'

'We? What do you mean, "we"? Look, Mr Harper, let me make this plain here and now, I have no intention of accepting the bequest. I never asked for it and frankly I don't *want* it. I have no idea why your grandfather chose to leave those shares to me, but I have every intention of refusing to accept them. The shares are yours by right, and when I can get back upstairs again to see Mr Swan then I shall make that quite plain to him.' Genevieve stood up, swaying slightly till she caught her balance. 'Now, if you'll be good enough to help me back to his office I can set the wheels in motion. H.R. Holdings is yours, and I don't want any part of it.'

'A noble sentiment, Miss Gray. One I applaud wholeheartedly, but I'm afraid it isn't going to be as easy as that,' he said softly, moving further into the room, his blue eyes locked to her pale face.

'What do you mean?' she demanded. A shiver raced through her trembling body and she hugged her arms tightly round herself to quell it.

'Simply that Grandfather intended you to have

those shares and he went out of his way to make his will watertight so that you couldn't refuse them. There's a string of conditions attached to the bequest, and we shall have to go into them at some time, but the main gist is that you cannot sell me the shares, make me a present of them, or even hand them over to me if we married. If you try to do any one of those things then not only will you forfeit your right to your half but I shall forfeit my right to the other half. So it appears that for the time being you're stuck with them.'

He smiled, a faint grimness in his eyes which in all truth Genevieve could appreciate. But it was ridiculous; she didn't want any part of Ross Harper's company!

'But I don't want them!' she cried.

'That's as may be. Frankly I find it just the tiniest bit strange that you're willing to refuse such a valuable windfall. However, whether you want the shares or not, they're yours until I can find some way to reclaim them. For now, though, Miss Gray, it seems as if we're destined to be partners.'

Partners! The word echoed round and round Genevieve's head as she stared at him, her face filled with a mounting horror. Partners. . .she and Ross Harper! What a terrifying prospect!

CHAPTER FIVE

'I'M SORRY, but I can't agree with that proposal.'

A sudden hush filled the room, stemming the noisy babble of male voices, and Genevieve felt the colour surge to her cheeks as all eyes turned towards her. For a moment she regretted having spoken her feelings aloud, but it was only the briefest of moments. There was no way she could agree to the board's proposal to demolish almost three full streets just to make a car park. It was quite wrong.

The conviction stiffened her backbone, made her able to turn her head and meet the cold blue eyes that were boring into her, with an outward show of composure. This was the first board meeting of H.R. Holdings that she had attended and she had meant to sit quietly at the end of the table and say nothing till it was over, but this was too important an issue to remain silent on. The trouble was, Ross Harper very obviously didn't agree with her!

For a long minute he stared at her, his handsome face as hard as granite, then he smiled, a curling, mocking tilt to his lips that warned Genevieve she was in for trouble.

'So, Miss Gray, you don't agree with the proposal. Does that mean that you intend to vote against it?' His blue eyes dared her to give the wrong answer, and all of a sudden Genevieve felt her temper flare up and almost choke her. He had been the one who had insisted that she should attend the meeting, the one who had sent a car to collect her, the one who had rudely informed her that it was her duty as a major shareholder to attend, so now he must take the consequences! Undoubtedly he had assumed that she would be overwhelmed by it all, would be willing to comply with all his decisions, but he'd been wrong. She was nobody's puppet! She had a mind of her own and she would use it, no matter how much it might upset him.

She sat up straighter and smiled calmly back at him, watching the faint annoyance on his face turn to anger as she said clearly,

'Yes. I shall vote against it.'

There was a sudden burst of conversation that reached a deafening crescendo before Ross Harper banged on the table, his clenched fist striking the polished surface with a force which only emphasised how angry he really was.

'Why?' he demanded. 'Why should you vote against it? What possible difference does it make to you whether we pull those wretched houses down or not? After all, you'll still get your dividends from the deal, and frankly they'll be far greater if we go ahead with the project. The new shopping arcade needs another car park as an overflow site from the main one. Without it some of our prospective tenants could try to back out. You, Miss Gray, are in danger of ruining the whole project!'

For a second Genevieve quailed at the thought, wondering if she was right to refuse. From what she had already learned during the meeting, this new arcade was costing the company millions. Surely she would be quite wrong to jeopardise its success, no matter what sort of gut feeling she had about the ethics of it.

Undecided, she glanced down the long table, her eyes running swiftly over the hostile faces of the other board members, and shivered. Not one of the men had spoken a word to her when she'd walked in that morning. They had greeted her with a cold and stony silence that proclaimed all too clearly what they thought of her presence there. News of the bequest had soon spread round the town; she had been plagued by telephone calls and even begging letters for the past week. George Roberts must have known what the reaction would be to the news, must have known how unpopular she would be in the male-dominated boardroom of H.R. Holdings, so why had he done it? Why had he left her those shares and so much power? He must have had some sort of solid reason for it, not just been taken by a sudden whim. Had this sort of situation been the reason behind it? Had he wanted her to bring a compassionate eye to what would normally be a purely business decision? With a sudden flash of insight Genevieve knew that she might have found the explanation for the unexpected bequest.

Well, she wouldn't let Mr Roberts down. She wouldn't allow this group of men to calmly decide to destroy people's homes just for the sake of an overflow car park! There was more to life than putting a monetary value on everything.

'I think you're overstating the importance of the car park, Mr Harper,' she said finally, her eyes meeting his boldly.

'Am I?' he asked softly. 'Am I indeed? And what do you base this feeling on, Miss Gray? Experience gained from running your shop, or feminine intuition?'

There was a rumble of appreciative laughter from the men sitting round the table at this thrust, and Genevieve clamped down on the host of spiky comments which were fighting to break free from her lips. How dared he mock her like that, speak to her as if she were some sort of imbecile? She forced herself to sit calmly waiting till the laughter died away, leaving a tense, uncomfortable silence behind it. Then she smiled, her face cold and filled with a contempt that brought a surge of angry colour to Ross Harper's cheeks.

'A definite point to you, Mr Harper, so notch it up. You're quite right, of course. I don't have any *real* experience of running a business at this level, but I do have one thing which you so obviously lack.'

'And what's that?' he bit out.

'The ability to judge a siutation from the public's point of view. How do you think it will look in the papers when word gets out? Can't you just see the headlines now, something along the lines of "Consortium makes people homeless for the sake of a car park." I'm sure that kind of publicity won't enhance H.R. Holdings' standing in the community. . .but then maybe that's not very important to a big company.'

Genevieve sat back in her seat, listening with a tiny smile on her lips as a hurried conversation broke out once again round the table. Suddenly a voice cut

through the noise and she glanced round to see who
was speaking.

'She's right, you know, Ross. The papers will
make a meal of it, especially as it will be just before
Christmas when we get round to the demolition. We
caught the flak last time from that office block, so
can't you picture it. H.R.'s made out to be the
modern-day Scrooge? It could cost us thousands in
goodwill.'

Graham Marriot, the company's chief accountant,
glanced sideways at Genevieve and smiled, and she
smiled back, glad to have found one ally at least.

'And what about all the thousands we'll lose if
anyone backs out at this stage? You know what the
multi-nationals are like about parking facilities. How
would we recoup that? It's just sentimental rubbish.'

'You call losing your home "sentimental rubbish"?' Genevieve shot back.

'Have you seen those houses? Well, have you?
Two up, two down monstrosities which should have
been pulled down years ago. They're not fit for
people to live in.'

'So why not do something about them?' demanded
Genevieve, her brown eyes hot with spiralling
temper. 'Lots of towns are going in for renovating
old property now, instead of pulling it down and
splitting up whole communities. Now that you own
the land and houses why not invest some money in
it, restore the houses, add on bathrooms, kitchens,
etc? Why, if half of them are already empty then
you'll stand to make a profit when you sell them
again. After all, with the new arcade being built and
property in the area being at a premium, you can't

fail, not to mention all the good publicity it will bring you.'

Graham Marriot whistled softly, his pleasant face holding a touch of admiration which was balm to Genevieve's bruised feelings. 'She's right, you know, Ross, absolutely right. Oh, admittedly it will cost a packet bringing the houses up to standard, but there are grants we can get to offset a major part of it, and the goodwill it will bring to the company if we handle it right is incalculable.'

'And what about the car park? We need it, need the extra space to bring in enough business for the major retailers.'

It was obvious that Ross Harper still wasn't prepared to give an inch and Genevieve wondered why he was being so completely pigheaded when it all made so much sense. She glanced towards him, studying the harsh set to his handsome face, the grim line to his lips, and in a sudden flash she realised that his refusal to be convinced stemmed from something far more personal. It wasn't just that what she'd said made sense, it was the fact that *she* had said it. He must dislike her very much to let personal feelings outweigh his judgement. The thought was oddly depressing.

She glanced down at her hands, feeling the hot prickle of tears sting at her lids. All of a sudden she felt drained, as though all the emotional turmoil she'd gone through in the past few weeks had sapped her energy, leaving her empty. The room and all the hostility seemed to be closing in on her and she knew she had to get out. She stood up, uncaring that a dozen pairs of eyes had turned on her. All she could feel was the cold dislike of a pair of icy blue ones.

'I'm sorry, but I've had enough for today. I realise that most of you resent me being here, resent the fact that I've been left the shares, but it's something which I can do nothing about. I just want to make it quite plain that while I retain control of them I shall do everything possible to ensure that H.R. Holdings uses its power in a way which will benefit not only the company but the community as well. Now, if you'll excuse me, I think it would be better if I left.'

Picking up her bag, Genevieve hurried from the room, keeping her eyes averted from Ross Harper as she passed him. She walked quickly along the corridor and pressed the button for the lift, feeling her legs trembling with reaction. She leant against the wall, closing her eyes to hold back the tears, her body stiffening as she heard the sound of approaching footsteps.

'I want a word with you. Come with me.'

Ross Harper took her arm and pulled her firmly after him, his long fingers tightening painfully as she dug in her heels and tried to resist.

'Let me go!'

Twisting round, she tried to break free, but she was powerless to escape his numbing hold. Dragging her like a reluctant puppy on the end of a lead, he steered her along the corridor and into his office, closing the door and leaning back against it before he let her go. Genevieve shot away from him and stopped in the middle of the room, rubbing her aching flesh with shaking fingers. She glared at him, hating the way he was standing there so coolly watching her, no hint of emotion of his face.

'Well, what do you want?' she demanded. 'What's so important that you need to drag me in here?'

'I'm sorry if I was a bit rough, but it was your own fault. All you had to do was come with me instead of causing such a commotion.'

'You'd cause a commotion if someone man-handled you!' she snapped back, trying to push a few loose strands of hair back into their neat french pleat. She opened her bag and took out a small mirror, holding it aloft while she attempted to tuck the silky ends back into place, but they kept slithering down round her flushed face. With a murmur of annoyance she dragged the pins out and shook her hair free, smoothing it back from her face and tucking it behind her dainty ears.

'Mmm, looks better like that, less severe and schoolmarmish.' Ross Harper was still leaning indolently back against the door, his jacket open, his hands thrust deep into the pockets of his well-fitting trousers, openly assessing her appearance, and Genevieve felt her simmering temper rise a little further.

'You can keep your comments to yourself,' she snapped waspishly. 'How I look has nothing whatsoever to do with you!'

'OK, OK, there's no need to start World War Three over it!' He held his hand up as though warding off imaginary bullets, and Genevieve turned away, annoyed with herself for reacting so violently to a passing comment. She walked over to the window and stared out, watching the traffic flowing past in the street as she tried to hang on to what little was left of her composure. If she wasn't careful she was in danger of making a complete and utter fool of herself.

She made herself count slowly up to ten, then turned back, her eyes drifting to the tall figure now sitting calmly behind the desk. She should have had the advantage now that he was sitting down and no longer towering over her, yet, surprisingly, it didn't feel that way at all. Standing or sitting, it was Ross Harper who was in command in that room.

Shaken by the realisation, Genevieve sat down abruptly on a nearby chair and stared at him, waiting to hear his reasons for bringing her into his office. As she watched he picked up a pen, sliding and twisting the slender length of it between his long fingers, and for a moment she wondered if he was nervous, before dismissing the idea as crazy. A man like Ross Harper wouldn't even know the meaning of nerves! He was made of granite, right through to the core.

He looked up, his blue eyes holding hers for a second before he spoke, his voice low yet strangely commanding. 'We have to come to some sort of agreement, Miss Gray. Confrontations like the one earlier are not only distressing but dangerous.'

'Dangerous. . .are you threatening me?'

'No, of course not. For heaven's sake stop jumping to conclusions, woman! They're dangerous because they unsettle the rest of the board, and that could prove to be very detrimental to the company. Between us we hold the controlling interest, but if one or two members of the board get wind of the fact that things are. . .well, strained between us, then it could prove to be a problem. There've been two attempts recently to take over control of the company, and frankly I've only been able to stave them off because my grandfather gave me his proxy vote. If there's even the faintest hint that we're at odds and can be divided then you can rest assured that someone will attempt to do it again.' He leant forward, his blue eyes burning with an intensity she'd never seen before. 'I have no intention of letting the company fall into outsiders' hands, Miss Gray. I shall do anything at all to stop it happening.'

There was a grimness in his deep voice that sent a shiver of cold dread racing through Genevieve's slender body. She clasped her hands tightly together and stared back at him, wondering what it was he wanted from her. Surely he hadn't just brought her in here for a pep talk, had he?

'You can appreciate the seriousness of my position, I hope, can understand that I need to avoid any sort of confrontation which will rock the boat. I won't go into details at the moment, but very shortly I mean to have enough shares in my name so that there'll be no danger of anyone else gaining control of the company. All I need is a couple of months' breathing space and I should be ready.'

'I appreciate your being so frank with me, but you must admit that you were partly to blame for this morning's little disagreement. Be honest, if anyone else but me had made the objection and suggestion about those houses, would you have been quite so ready to dismiss it?'

He shrugged, a faint, self-mocking smile on his

lips that stirred something to unwilling life inside
Genevieve as she saw it.

'Possibly, possibly not. If we're being honest then
I have to admit that my reaction was influenced by
the fact that it was you who made the point. If it had
been someone else, well. . .' He spread his hands
wide in a gesture of defeat, and Genevieve felt
herself warm to him a trifle. At least he had the
grace to admit that he could have been in the wrong.
It was a small step along the rocky road towards
them finding some sort of common ground to work
on.

She leant towards him across the desk, her eyes
dark with sincerity.

'Look, Mr Harper, I can understand how upset
you've been by this whole business. It must have
been a tremendous shock to discover that Mr
Roberts had left the shares to me, but I shall do
everything in my power to help you, to support you
in the business.'

'Anything?' he repeated softly. 'Anything at all?'

She drew back abruptly, something about the tone
of his deep voice making her instantly wary. 'Well,
yes. . .within reason, of course,' she qualified
quickly. He was watching her now with an
expression in his eyes that bothered her, though she
couldn't really say why. She sat up rigidly straight in
the chair, twisting her hands tightly in her lap, hating
to ask the next question, but knowing that she had
to.

'What is it that you want me to do, Mr Harper?'

There was a tiny pause, a split second of absolute
silence, and she had the sudden craziest feeling that

she was sitting on top of a powder keg waiting for the explosion. Yet nothing on this earth could have prepared her for the shock when he lit the fuse.

'It's very simple, Miss Gray. You and I are already partners, but it's not enough. We need to be closer than that, far closer.'

'Closer?' she echoed, her eyes widening. 'Wh— what do you mean?'

'Lovers,' he said succinctly. 'You and I need to be lovers. It's the only way to safeguard the company.'

He'd gone mad, stark, staring mad from the shock of what had happened over the shares! That was the only explanation for it.

With a murmured cry Genevieve leapt to her feet, her face flushed, her eyes wide with a mounting horror as she stared at Ross Harper, who was sitting calmly watching her reaction. She opened her mouth, desperately trying to find something to say, some cutting comment, something equal to the occasion, but frankly there was nothing she could come up with!

'I. . .I. . .'

'Sit down, Miss Gray. Once again you've jumped to the wrong conclusion.'

'Wrong conclusion? How on earth have I jumped to the wrong conclusion? You made yourself very clear. Lovers was the word you used, and I have a very good idea of what that means!' She glared down at him, her eyes burning, her cheeks stained a hectic carmine.

'Have you indeed, and does the thought of us like that bother you so much, then?' His voice was a mere whisper of soft sound in the tense silence and

for some reason Genevieve found that she couldn't
look away from his penetrating gaze. Warmth stole
through her body, curled deep in the very pit of her
stomach at the picture his words invoked of them
together. . .as lovers.

For a full minute they stayed locked into a cocoon
of silence, then finally Genevieve found the strength
to look away. She swallowed hard, forcing herself to
breathe slowly and steadily, to wipe away the tantalising, debilitating images. Ross Harper didn't really
want her, as a woman; he wanted her as a shareholder, a safeguard for his business. The knowledge
made her go suddenly cold all over.

'Mr Harper——'

'Please sit down, Miss Gray. We're only wasting
time bandying words like this. I shall explain exactly
what my proposal is and then you can tell me
whether you'll agree to go along with it.'

The cold ice in his deep voice steadied her, and
rather to her surprise she found herself obeying the
command. She sat back down on the chair, her
hands neatly folded in her lap, her eyes fixed on a
spot just above his head. She didn't want to look at
him, didn't want him to see just how much that brief
moment of madness had shaken her.

'First of all, let me say that I've thought long and
hard about this for the past couple of weeks. No,
hear me out.' He held his hand up as Genevieve
started to interrupt him, and she fell silent. 'However, when I made that suggestion to you before I
never meant that it should be anything other than an
act, a pretence solely for the benefit of outsiders.
The world, and, more importantly, the board of

H.R. Holdings, needs to believe that we're united, that it's impossible to divide us or our vote.'

'But surely it would be far simpler to make sure that we always try to agree on things? Why do we need to go through with such a ridiculous charade?' Genevieve's voice was a trifle high-pitched, and she drew in a deep breath to stem the panic rising inside her.

'It would be marvellous if we could do that, but do you really believe it's possible, that we can work together in perfect harmony with never a cross word? No, we need to foster a deeper relationship between us, one that links us together despite any trivial disagreements we might have. A romantic attachment would be perfect, a real bond between us which it would be difficult for anyone to break.'

'Oh, yes?' There was irony in Genevieve's voice. 'And just who will believe that any romantic attachment you form will last, Ross Harper? With your track record!'

'Isn't there a saying about reformed rakes?' he asked with a low laugh that sent a delicious tingle coursing down Genevieve's backbone. 'Oh, I'm quite certain that people will believe it if we try hard enough to convince them.'

'What do you mean, "try hard"? Look, I'm willing to concede that you might, just might, be right, but there's no way I'm going to be talked into an affair with you just for the sake of the business! I want to know exactly what it will all entail and how long we'll be expected to keep up the pretence.'

'A couple of months, three at the most. I've already got people buying up shares for me, and word has gone out that a sizeable block will be coming on to the market soon, so it's really only a question of waiting for the right moment. All I want you to do is be seen with me in all the right places, making certain that everyone believes we're inseparable. It will give me the bit of breathing space I need. I know it's a lot to ask, but I'm sure my grandfather never intended that I should lose control of the company.'

It was pure emotional blackmail, Genevieve acknowledged the fact, yet she was powerless to resist it as her conscience rose up and sided with him. She couldn't allow H.R. Holdings to slip from his control because of a bequest she really wasn't entitled to. She nodded, her eyes still faintly troubled as they met his.

Ross smiled at her, his handsome face settling into lines of relief which made her realise just how worried he had been. He stood up and came round the desk, holding his hands out, and slowly Genevieve slid her fingers into his and let him draw her to her feet.

'Thank you, Genevieve,' he said softly. 'You won't regret it.' Bending his dark head, he brushed his lips gently over the soft curve of her cheek, and she shuddered at the brief contact. She drew back, staring down at their linked hands, wondering why she almost wished it weren't a pretence but real; that she and Ross Harper really would be lovers!

The thought shocked her so much that she pulled away abruptly and picked up her bag which had fallen to the floor, using the few seconds to re-gather her composure. She couldn't afford to let him see what she was feeling, because he would use it to his advantage. From what he had just told her he would do anything to safeguard H.R. Holdings. It was the only thing he really cared about. To allow herself to become attracted to him was courting trouble, opening herself up to a hurt which instinct warned her would be greater than any she had ever suffered. There could be nothing between her and this man but a business arrangement: both common sense and the terms of the will precluded any other kind of relationship.

She drew in a deep breath, her face strangely blank when she turned back to him.

'When do you want to start this pretence?'

'As soon as possible.' He walked back round the desk and sat down, his dark head bent as he studied a big leather-bound diary. For a moment Genevieve stared down at him, feeling a tiny ache flare into life inside her, as though something precious had been lost to her for ever. Ross looked up, his face coolly impersonal, and she brushed the crazy little feeling aside, knowing she couldn't afford to weaken.

'How about Friday,' he asked quietly.

'This. . .this Friday?' There was a husky note to her soft voice, the tiniest tremor which no amount of willpower could level out, and he smiled, his face almost kindly.

'Yes, this Friday. There really is no point in waiting, is there, Genevieve? We have to try and establish our relationship as soon as possible, and Friday would be the perfect opportunity. We should get maximum exposure.'

'Where are we going, then?'

'The Lord Mayor's Summer Ball. I wasn't going to bother attending this year, but frankly it would be ideal. There's always extensive Press coverage and all the local business community will be there, along with most of H.R.'s board members.'

'But do you think they'll buy it, that we're—well, going out together? I mean, this morning it was open warfare, so surely they'll find it rather strange seeing us together all nice and cosy so soon?' There was open disbelief on Genevieve's softly flushed face, but obviously Ross didn't share her concern. He smiled confidently at her, not the faintest trace of doubt in his blue eyes.

'Oh, I'm quite sure they'll get the picture by the end of the evening. Just leave it to me!'

What could she say to that? Genevieve stared at him, swallowing down the protest which had sprung to her lips. She had agreed to his proposal and there was no way she could now make a fuss and refuse to carry on with it.

'Well, is that a date, then?'

'Yes.' Her voice was no more than a croak of sound and she coughed, hating him to know just how shaken she felt by the prospect of the coming evening. 'What time do you want me to meet you, and what shall I wear? Is it a very formal occasion?'

'I'll pick you up, of course, round seven, and it's definitely a black tie affair, so dress accordingly. Here, I'll give you a cheque so that you can get yourself something.'

He pulled a cheque-book out of the desk drawer and picked up his pen, his hand halting as Genevieve said coldly, every word dripping with ice, 'There's

TAKE 4 MEDICAL ROMANCES FREE

Mills & Boon Medical Romances capture the excitement, intrigue and emotion of the busy medical world. A world often interrupted by love and romance...

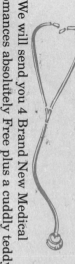

We will send you 4 Brand New Medical Romances absolutely Free plus a cuddly teddy bear and a surprise mystery gift, as your introduction to this superb series.

At the same time we'll reserve a subscription for you to our Reader Service. Every two months you could receive the 6 latest Medical Romances delivered direct to your door Post and Packing Free, plus a free Newsletter packed with competitions, author news and much, much more.

What's more there's no obligation, you can cancel or suspend your subscription at any time. So you've nothing to lose and a whole world of romance to gain!

Your Free Gifts!

We'll send you this cute little tan and white teddy bear plus a surprise mystery gift when you return this card. So don't delay.

Fill in the Free Books Coupon overleaf ▶▶

Free Books Certificate

Yes! Please send me my 4 Free Medical Romances, together with my Free Teddy and Mystery gift. Please also reserve a special Reader Service subscription for me. If I decide to subscribe, I shall receive 6 superb new books every two months for just £8.10, post and packaging free. If I decide not to subscribe, I shall write you within 10 days. The free books and gifts will be mine to keep in any case.

I understand that I am under no obligation whatsoever - I can cancel or suspend my subscription at any time simply by writing to you.

I am over 18 years of age.

Extra Bonus

We all love surprises, so as well as the Free books and Teddy, here's an intriguing mystery gift especially for you. No clues - send off today!

Mrs/Miss/Ms _____
(BLOCK CAPITALS PLEASE)

Address _____

_____

_____ Postcode _____ 5AOD

Signature _____

NO STAMP NEEDED

Reader Service
FREEPOST
PO Box 236
Croydon
Surrey
CR9 9EL

Send No Money Now

no need for that. I am quite capable of finding something suitable to wear for the occasion. Don't worry, I shall do my best not to let you down!'

She glared at him, her face filled with an icy anger that he should insult her in such a manner. Admittedly, she was hardly in the usual category of his rich girlfriends, but she wasn't a pauper either. She didn't need a hand-out, thank you!

'I'm sorry, I didn't mean to offend you,' he said quietly, studying her set face. 'I just didn't want you to be out of pocket in any way. After all, you're doing this at my request and for the sake of the company. Why not view it in terms of expenses?'

He made sense in a way, yet Genevieve was still too annoyed by the deeper implications of the offer to be mollified. She tossed her hair back from her face, slipping it behind her ears with shaking fingers.

'I want you to understand just one thing, Mr Harper. Your grandfather might have left me those shares and there might be nothing I can do about it at present, but there's no way I intend to profit from the bequest. Those shares are yours by right and I won't accept a penny of either yours or the company's money.'

'Why not?' he asked, his face filled with a mounting disbelief. 'Frankly, I find it very strange that you're so unwilling to accept the bequest. No one is that altruistic. In your place I'd be trying to milk the company for every penny.'

'Oh, I can believe that, but there again, that's where you and I differ. The money just isn't that important to me. I agree that lack of it's a problem, but having money just for the sake of it isn't one of my goals in life. I like to earn what I get, to know that what I have is mine by dint of hard work. Money isn't one of my gods.'

'How very noble of you! I only wish I could believe half of it.'

Even without the irony in his voice Genevieve would have known he didn't believe a word she'd said. She turned away and hurried towards the door, feeling strangely hurt by his reaction to her honesty.

'Oh, by the way, Miss Gray, I shall expect you to keep the details of our agreement completely secret. I don't want to hear even a whisper that everything might not be quite how it seems.'

She swung round, her hand resting on the door-handle, her brown eyes filled with scorn as she stared back at him across the width of the room.

'Don't worry, Mr Harper. I wouldn't want my best friend to know that I was in league with *you*!'

She walked out of the room, closing the door quietly behind her, hugging the memory of his furious face to her like a comforter. It was the only good memory out of a wretched and miserable day.

CHAPTER SIX

GENEVIEVE cut a long length of the brilliant red ribbon and twisted it into a huge bow before pinning it carefully to the cellophane wrapping of the bouquet.

'Gen. . .are you still here? I thought you'd have left ages ago. Just look at the time! It's gone five already.'

Cathy stood in the doorway, her usually cheerful face filled with concern as she squinted short-sightedly up at the wall clock, and Genevieve sighed. Reluctantly she set the bouquet aside and stood up, wiping her hands on a cloth lying on the counter. Cathy was right, it was getting late and she really should have left the shop at least an hour earlier, yet somehow she'd been trying to stave off the inevitable moment a while longer.

'I'm just going,' she said, smiling with a false strained brightness at her assistant. 'I just wanted to finish this last order off before I left.'

'Well, leave the rest to me,' ordered Cathy, picking up the flowers and holding them firmly as though frightened Genevieve might change her mind. 'Honestly, Gen, if I were going out with Ross Harper you wouldn't see me for dust! I'd have spent the whole afternoon prinking and preening myself just for the occasion.'

Cathy's eyes were wide with excitement, and

Genevieve wished she could share the feeling with her. The closer the time came to when she must meet that man again, the more terrified she felt. Why had she allowed him to talk her into it, allowed that irritating noisy conscience of hers to side with him? She should have refused to have anything at all to do with him and his rotten plan. What did she care what happened to H.R. Holdings? It would serve him right if he lost control of the whole damned company, because if ever a man deserved his come-uppance it was him!

Her mind seething with nasty thoughts and evil wishes, she gave Cathy instructions about locking up and left. She took her time, idling along the summer-warm streets as she made her way home to the tall grey stone building where she rented her flat. Letting herself in the front door, she skipped smartly up the stairs, anxious not to cross paths with anyone along the way. She didn't feel in the mood for swapping polite conversation with anyone tonight. She just wanted to concentrate all her thoughts on the coming ordeal.

Reaching the third floor, she hurried along the corridor, her heart sinking as a door opened and her next-door neighbour came out. Genevieve smiled at her, scrabbling in her bag for the key, her fingers all clumsy thumbs in her haste to get inside before Jackie could stop her. Despite the fact that they had rented flats next door to each other for almost a year now, it was only in the past few weeks that the other girl had bothered to speak to her. Genevieve had the uncharitable feeling that her sudden bequest had been the reason behind Jackie's change in attitude.

'Hi, Gen. Looks as if you're in a hurry. Here, let me get that for you.'

Jackie bent down to retrieve the key and half the contents of the bag, which had slipped from her fumbling fingers, and Genevieve murmured her thanks before hastily opening the flat door. She glanced quickly at her watch, aware that she had cut things rather fine by dawdling if she intended to have a bath and wash her hair before Ross arrived. She would have to get a move on.

She turned round, ready to dismiss her neighbour with a smile and a few carefully chosen words which wouldn't invite any further conversation, but Jackie out-manoeuvred her with the ease of long practice. Whipping round the door, she slid into the flat, smiling warmly at Genevieve as she took the door from her and closed it.

'Now come on, tell me where you're off to.' She sat down on the sofa, calmly ignoring the cold look Genevieve shot at her, an expression of avid curiosity on her skilfully made-up features. Genevieve sighed, admitting defeat as she dumped her bag on one of the coffee tables. There was really no way she could bring herself to be openly rude to the other girl.

'The Summer Ball.'

'Oh, wow, how marvellous! You lucky thing!' There was envy in Jackie's voice and in the quick glance she ran over Genevieve as though trying to assess why she warranted an invitation to such a prestigious event. 'Who's taking you?'

Well, that really was the biggie, wasn't it? Genevieve chewed on her lip, somehow loath to admit who was to be her escort for the evening, yet what was the point in avoiding it? If Ross was right then the whole city would know that she'd been out with him by the morning.

'Ross Harper,' she said flatly, kicking off her sandals and deliberately avoiding the other girl's startled, disbelieving glance.

'Did you say Ross Harper?'

Genevieve smiled and shrugged, trying to make light of the fact that the most eligible bachelor in town was her escort for the evening. . .and for several months to come, a tiny voice reminded her.

'Well, well, you are moving in exalted circles, aren't you? What's he like? As gorgeous as he looks in the papers?'

Jackie settled back on the sofa and Genevieve realised she wasn't going to get rid of her without satisfying some of her curiosity. She thought quickly, deliberately forcing a warmly intimate little smile to her soft lips.

'Ross is. . .well, unbelievable.'

'I'll bet he is!'

Mercifully Jackie missed the irony behind the words and saw only what she wanted to. She stared up at Genevieve, her rather hard green eyes filled with a greedy curiosity. 'How long have you known him, Gen? Since the will, when you were left all that lovely money?'

Her tone suggested that must be the only reason for her knowing a man in Ross Harper's elevated position, and Genevieve took instant offence to it. OK, so she wasn't beautiful, but she was hardly so ugly that she couldn't have attracted him without the lure of the shares! Totally ignoring the fact that that was the real reason he had asked her out, she replied shortly, 'Ross and I have known each other for some time now. Long before his grandfather died, in fact.'

It was only the smallest embellishment of the truth, after all, and quite justified in the circumstances. She had known him before, though not in the way the worldly Jackie probably meant.

'Oh, I see. Funny it never got into the papers, though, isn't it? I mean, whatever that man does usually hits the society columns at some point. I rather think they hold space just for him.'

Well, in for a penny, in for a pound, and that note of doubt in the other girl's voice was irritating.

'Ross has a house in the country as well as a flat in town. We met there rather than have people gossiping about us.'

'Did you indeed? Well, well, you are dark horse, aren't you, Gen, a really dark horse.'

'Not really. I just like to keep my private life private, if you know what I mean.'

'Oh, I do, I do, and you can trust me not to breathe a word to a living soul!'

Well, if she believed that then she would believe anything! Jackie was an inveterate gossip, but Genevieve wasn't prepared to argue the point. Time was marching on and if she didn't get a move on she would never be ready in time.

'Thanks, Jackie, I appreciate that. Now, I'm sorry to rush you, but I really must get ready.'

'Sure. What time is he collecting you, by the way?'

The question was asked so casually that Genevieve answered it without thinking, then could have bitten her tongue off as she saw the speculative gleam in Jackie's eyes.

'Seven.'

'Seven, eh? Well, I'd better let you get on. See you, Gen. Have fun!'

With a careless wave of her hand Jackie hurried out, leaving Genevieve staring after her, feeling as though she'd just committed some act of incredible folly. Why had she told her what time Ross was coming? Knowing Jackie, she'd find some reason to call in just to meet him. Still, there was nothing she could do about it now. It served her right for being so foolishly touchy about their arrangement. If Jackie said anything to Ross, let drop the fact that she knew they'd been having some sort of relationship before Mr Roberts' death, then she would die of embarrassment!

Desperate to push such an unsettling thought aside, Genevieve hurried round getting ready for the evening. She had a bath and washed her hair in near-record time, then sat wrapped in a bath-towel while she blew her hair dry. She had intended to curl it for the occasion, but one swift glance at the small clock on her bedside table put paid to that idea. It was already turning six-thirty, far too late to be struggling with rollers and tongs at this late hour.

Contenting herself with brushing the silky length of hair until it fell like pale satin round her neck and shoulders, she set to work on her make-up, determined that she was going to present the best picture possible to Ross. When she had finished she sat back and studied herself critically, feeling rather pleased with the effect. Careful use of eye-pencil and shadow had made her brown eyes look even bigger than they were already, the soft, muted colours she'd chosen enhancing the golden flecks in their depths. A soft pale rose lipstick made her mouth look lush and inviting, the delicate shade warming the pale olive tint of her smooth complexion. All that was needed now was a spray of her very best perfume and when she was dressed she would be ready to face anything. . .even Ross Harper!

Genevieve picked up the crystal vial and sprayed a fine mist behind her ears and down the smooth sweep of her neck to the deep V between her full breasts. The perfume had been a wicked extravagance which she had allowed herself the last time she'd travelled over to France to visit her mother, but, sniffing the delicious, heady aroma, Genevieve knew that it was money well spent. She'd eaten beans on toast for two weeks after making the impulsive purchase, but frankly, every single stodgy mouthful had been worth it!

Smiling to herself, she crossed the room and slid open the wardrobe doors, lifting out the dress she intended to wear that night. She held it up, her eyes sweeping critically down the front of the long, soft skirt, and nodded in satisfaction. Made of pale cream silk, the dress was a designer model, with a tight-fitting strapless bodice and long full skirt which just brushed her ankles. New it must have cost a small fortune, yet Genevieve had paid just a couple of pounds for it at a rummage sale held in aid of one of the local Brownie packs.

When she had first unearthed it from the heap of crumpled clothing and seen the huge wine stain

marring one side of the long skirt, she had almost
tossed it aside again. However, with some idea of
cutting it up for cushion covers, she had decided to
buy it, wondering if she was only wasting two
precious pounds she could ill afford to lose. Some
impulse had made her try it on when she got home,
and she had been completely taken aback to find
that it fitted her perfectly and just how much the
creamy colour suited her golden colouring.

Genevieve had always been skilful with a needle,
an art her mother had taught her, and she had spent
the whole of that evening unpicking the skirt from
the bodice to see if there was any way she could cut
out the stained patch of material. There were yards
of rich creamy silk in the skirt, and with skill and
patience she had been able to do it. It had taken her
hour upon hour of delicate, careful sewing but,
viewing the restored and now beautiful dress, she
knew that it had been worth all the effort. The gown
looked a million dollars; no one would ever guess
just how little it had cost her!

Humming softly to herself, she unwrapped the
damp towel and let it fall to the floor, falling silent
as the doorbell suddenly rang, its noise echoing
round the quiet flat. Wide-eyed with alarm, she
glanced at the small clock to check the time, her
heart racing wildly with anxiety. Surely it couldn't
be Ross yet, could it? There were still ten minutes
left before he was due to collect her.

For a whole minute she stood rooted to the spot
till another peal of the bell galvanised her into
action. She scurried round, frantically trying to find
her robe, before suddenly remembering that it was

in the laundry hamper waiting to be washed. She shot a hunted look at the wisps of lace underwear lying on the bed, trying to assess just how quickly she could slip them on and get dressed, but another louder ringing of the bell plus a heavy pounding on the wooden panels forced her to accept the fact that she would never manage it in time. If her caller kept up that sort of racket much longer then he would have everyone coming to see what was happening!

Snatching up the soggy towel, she wrapped it firmly round herself and hurried to answer the door, wondering what sort of nasty fate had made this happen. She had meant to be dressed and ready well before Ross arrived so that she wouldn't have to ask him inside, but now there was little she could do about it. She couldn't leave him standing outside on the landing, not after all she'd said to Jackie. It would make a mockery of everything she'd told her!

With shaking fingers Genevieve unlocked the door and edged it open just the barest fraction to stare up at the tall man standing outside. In a slow sweep her eyes ran over him from head to toe, a reluctant admiration in their depths. Dressed in a black dinner suit and snowy linen, with his dark hair sleekly brushed and his tanned skin glowing, he looked so absolutely stunning that for a moment Genevieve was totally lost for words to say to such an apparition of male beauty. Then he smiled, the familiar hint of mockery curling his lips, and the illusion was shattered.

'Good evening, Genevieve.'

'You're early,' Genevieve snapped back, a trifle

waspishly. 'It's barely ten to seven and I'm not ready!'

'So I see,' he murmured softly. For a second his glittering gaze traced over the naked curve of her shoulders before sliding downwards, and she felt the betraying colour flood to her face before she could stop it. She looked quickly away, feeling the blood pounding and racing round her veins in a furious surge that left her trembling. Though she hated to admit it, it wasn't embarrassment that she felt when he looked at her that way, but sheer physical attraction!

Stepping back from the door, she opened it further, tightening her grip on the front of the towel as he brushed past her. She closed the door, her hand lingering against the cold lock for a second longer than was really necessary, needing the feel of its solidity to add reality to the situation. It seemed so incredible that all this should be happening, that she should be inviting the most eligible bachelor in town into her flat while dressed only in a damp bath-towel, that it was difficult not to think she was dreaming.

She turned round slowly, a tiny tremor of sensation rippling through her as she saw the way Ross was studying the smooth bare length of her legs with obvious appreciation.

'I. . .er. . .I won't be long. Pour yourself a drink, if you want one. There's sherry and Scotch over there on the table.' She swept a hand towards the small polished-wood table standing between the two narrow windows which overlooked the rear garden, her cheeks turning fiery as the towel slipped a good few inches, threatening what little was left of her modesty. She snatched it upwards, her fingers tightening on the rough fabric. 'I'd better get dressed or we'll be late.'

'There's no rush, really. Why don't we have that drink together and work out our tactics for the evening?'

'I'm hardly dressed for that,' Genevieve shot back, her eyes sparking.

'You're hardly dressed. . .period,' Ross retorted with a low chuckle of intimate laughter. 'But why worry? I'm sure we'll find it conducive to getting to know one another even faster!'

'Now listen here. . .' Genevieve began, then suddenly realised just how ridiculously out of hand the situation was getting. How could she hope to make him take her seriously when she was standing there nearly naked!

She swung round on her heel and stalked back into the bedroom, closing the door firmly behind her, aware that her whole body was trembling with a fine, tight tension. She closed her eyes, willing herself to be calm, to ignore Ross's maddening, pointed comments, but it was incredibly difficult to do that, incredibly difficult to erase the memory of how his eyes had lingered with such appreciation on her body.

Suddenly, from out of nowhere, came the feeling that she was playing with fire by agreeing to this plan. Ross Harper was an expert on women. He must have honed his technique to absolute perfection over the years; how could she ever hope to withstand him if he used that technique on her?

Granted, she'd had her share of boyfriends and knew enough to cope with most things, yet never before had she experienced this wild, crazy excitement, this tingle of awareness she felt when Ross looked at her. She was no match for this man in the love game, no match at all.

Lost in thought, she dressed quickly in the lacy undies and slid the dress over her head, feeling slightly better once she had some sort of cover for her nakedness. She twisted an arm behind her back and slid the zipper up, muttering crossly as it snagged a couple of inches below the top of the brief tight bodice. Gently she tried to ease it down again to free the trapped fabric, but it refused to move either up or down and she was terrified that any rough handling would tear the delicate silk. There was no way she could work it free by herself. She would have to ask Ross to do it for her.

Holding the front of the dress against her bosom, Genevieve opened the bedroom door and walked out into the lounge, wishing the ground would open up and swallow her. Of all the embarrassing things to happen, and tonight of all times!

Ross was sitting quietly on the sofa, leafing through a magazine and sipping a glass of whisky. He set the glass aside and stood up when Genevieve came in, his eyes openly assessing her appearance.

'Beautiful,' he said softly. 'You look really beautiful, Genevieve. I wouldn't have thought you could have improved on your previous outfit, but frankly, that dress is perfect.'

The obviously sincere compliment bothered Genevieve more than she cared to admit, but she tried to make light of it by making a joke out of her predicament.

'Well, perhaps it will be perfect in a minute or so, that's if you can work this zipper loose. It seems to be jammed on a fold in the fabric. Would you mind looking at it for me?'

She turned round, presenting the smooth sweep of her bare back to him, glad that she didn't have to face him.

'Of course.'

In two long strides he crossed the room, his cool fingers brushing lightly against her skin as he carefully tried to separate the catch from the soft cloth. Genevieve shivered at the brief contact. She held herself rigid, only too aware of the heat of his body, the warm, soft flow of his breath against the nape of her neck as he bent closer. She closed her eyes, clutching hold of the front of the dress with tense fingers, desperately trying to remember that this was Ross Harper, a man whose lifestyle she had always viewed before with loathing. Yet, somehow, it seemed terribly difficult to quell the debilitating rush of sensation with pure common sense!

'Ah—right, I think I've got it.' With a deft gentle tug, Ross worked the zipper free, easing it down a couple of inches to smooth the fabric back into place. 'Now, just let me make sure it doesn't catch again. I'd hate to tear it.'

He slid his fingers into the back of the dress, resting them against Genevieve's skin as he drew the zip slowly upwards, and Genevieve bit her lip to stem the moan of appreciation at the exquisite feeling of his hand tracing up her backbone. For a second she stayed exactly where she was, too weak and shaken by the force of the feeling to move an inch, then slowly stepped away.

'Thank you.' Her voice was low, a faint huskiness to the soft tones, and Ross smiled at her gently, his eyes unfathomable.

'My pleasure, Genevieve.'

For a moment they stood and stared at each other, a strange wild tension gripping them both, charging the very atmosphere so that the world seemed to shiver on its axis and grind to a halt. Then a sudden knocking at the door broke the spell.

Genevieve turned away, her breath coming in short little bursts, feeling shaken to the core by the intensity of the moment they had just shared. She crossed the room to answer the door, scarcely aware of what she was doing, her body set on automatic pilot. The rest of her, the living breathing heart of her, was still locked in that magical timeless moment. However, one swift glance at the girl standing in the hallway soon restored her to her senses with a sickening jolt.

'Sorry to bother you, Gen,' said Jackie, smiling sweetly at her while her eyes slid past to rest on Ross. 'I was wondering if I could borrow some sugar.'

'Sugar?' Genevieve repeated blankly.

'Yes, sugar. I'm. . .I'm going to do some baking.'

Open-mouthed, Genevieve stared at this vision of domesticity, her startled eyes sweeping rapidly over the perfectly coiffured hair, down the silky crêpe-de-Chine dress to the four-inch-high lizardskin sandals, before finally halting on the long gold-lacquered nails. Baking! She had to be kidding. It was doubtful if Jackie even knew how to butter a slice of bread, let alone bake anything!

A chuckle of laughter bubbled up inside her and she looked hurriedly away, terrified that Jackie would see it. 'Of course. How much do you need?'

'Oh, a pound or so. Whatever you can spare.' With a charmingly vague wave of her hand Jackie stepped past her into the flat and smiled at Ross. 'Hi, I'm Jackie Webster, Gen's neighbour. I've been dying to meet you. Gen has told me so much about you.'

'Has she indeed?'

Ross took her outstretched hand, a cold gleam in his eyes as he shot a swift glance over the top of her head to Genevieve, who was standing watching. 'I hope it's been something nice.'

Jackie laughed, a practised, tinkly little laugh that set Genevieve's teeth on edge, and let her hand rest in Ross's for longer than was strictly necessary. 'How could it be otherwise?'

'How indeed? I just hope she hasn't give too many of our little secrets away.'

There was a note of menace in his deep voice yet, strangely, Jackie seemed to be totally unaware of it as she gazed alluringly up at him. Genevieve heard it, though, and stood up straighter, bristling at the implication. Obviously Ross was wondering exactly what she'd told her neighbour about their arrangement, but if he thought he could bully her into toeing the line then he could think again! No one told her how to act or what to do or what to

say. . .no one on God's green earth, and *that*
included Mr Wonderful Ross Harper!

With a low murmur she hurried into the kitchen,
terrified that she would say something she shouldn't
if she stayed in the same room as him a moment
longer. She poured half a bag of sugar into a plastic
tub, then snapped the lid back into place with a
vicious little push. She walked back into the
lounge—and stopped, her soft mouth curling with
distaste as she took in the scene.

Jackie was sitting next to Ross on the sofa, so
close that it would have been impossible to slip a
single sheet of paper between them. Her hand was
resting lightly on his arm while she stared up at him,
giving him the full benefit of two pairs of fluttering
false eyelashes. For a nasty moment Genevieve
hoped he would catch a chill from the draught they
were creating. He looked so engrossed in what
Jackie was saying, yet surely he could see what she
was really like, how false all that girlish sweetness
was? Still, what was it to her? They were welcome
to each other; in fact, viewed objectively, they were
probably perfect for each other. The man-eater and
the womaniser. . .what a wonderful match!

Something of her feelings must have shown in her
expression because when Ross glanced up and saw
her his face suddenly tightened. Aware that she had
lost his attention, Jackie stopped in mid-flow, a
flicker of annoyance crossing her face as she spotted
Genevieve standing in the doorway before she
quickly blanked it out.

'Oh, thanks, Gen. You are a love. I don't know
what I'd do without you.'

She stood up gracefully, smoothing the dress down over her slender hips, smiling faintly as Ross watched her. 'Well, have a lovely evening, both of you. It's been a pleasure meeting you, Mr Harper.'

'And you, Miss Webster.' Ross stood up, responding with a formal politeness to her, his mouth smiling while his eyes held a chilling bleakness that made Genevieve shiver.

'Oh, please, call me Jackie.'

'Thank you, and you must call me Ross, of course.'

Jackie smiled at him, a touch of triumph on her face as she sashayed out of the flat, leaving Genevieve to close the door behind her. There was a brief tense silence, then Ross spoke, his voice hard with a barely contained anger.

'What the hell have you been telling her?'

'Jackie? Nothing much. Why?'

Genevieve bent down to pick up her bag and check the contents, though she knew exactly what was in it down to the last ten pence and safety-pin.

'Are you sure you haven't been sounding off about our arrangement?'

She snapped the bag shut and looped it over her shoulder, shivering as the cold gilt chain touched her bare skin. 'I haven't told anyone about what we've planned, and frankly, the last person I would dream of telling would be her!'

Ross seemed to relax a trifle as he heard the scornful note of truth in her voice, the tension easing out of his big body. 'Doesn't sound as if you like her much, yet she gave me the impression that you were close friends. "Confidantes" was the word she used.'

Genevieve snorted with disgust and picked up the cobwebby square of gold lace she meant to use as a wrap. 'Jackie has a vivid imagination. Ignore her.'

Ross stepped forward and took the delicate web of fabric out of her hands, shaking it out gently before smoothing it slowly round her shoulders. For a second he stared deep into her eyes, a hint of curiosity on his face. 'So why did you tell her that you'd been to my flat and the house?'

Caught in the sticky web of her own lies, Genevieve couldn't think of a single reply but the truth. 'Because she implied that the idea of us going out together was ridiculous, that you would never have asked me if it hadn't been for the shares.'

'And you didn't like that?' he queried gently, his voice almost hypnotic in its soft depth.

She shook her head, her eyes huge and troubled. 'No.'

He smiled, a faint hint of satisfaction on his face. 'I'm glad. Now come along, let's go. The world is waiting for us, Genevieve Gray, so let's not disappoint it!'

He took her arm to lead her from the flat, and Genevieve let him, her mind only partly on what was happening. The rest of it was remembering his expression, that faint but unmistakable gleam of triumph, yet for the life of her she couldn't understand what had caused it.

CHAPTER SEVEN

'MISS GENEVIEVE GRAY and Mr Ross Harper.'

The major-domo made the announcement, and Genevieve went rigid as a hundred pairs of eyes seemed to focus in their direction. For a whole minute her mind went numb, refusing to give the right signals to her legs to make them move forward. Ross took her arm, his fingers tightening slightly round her bare flesh.

'Come on. Stick with me, kid, and you'll be all right!'

The hammed-up ganster impersonation made Genevieve giggle, and she relaxed immediately and let him lead her forward to shake hands with the Lord Mayor and other assorted dignitaries lined up to greet the guests. There was a polite exchange, a few brief pleasantries, then they were free to move on into the ballroom. Taking her arm, Ross steered her through the throng, nodding to people as he went, and Genevieve could feel the full power of a concentrated stare of curiosity boring into her.

Colour crept up her cheeks and she set her head at a regal angle as she crossed the room, refusing to be deterred by a single one of the assessing looks. She could almost hear the whispers which followed their progress, feel the scarcely veiled scrutiny of the other women as they viewed her from top to toe, and she muttered under her breath for Ross's ears alone, 'Why didn't you warn me it would be this bad?'

'Because you would never have come!'

There was laughter in his voice, and Genevieve smiled as she heard it, admitting that he was right. If she'd had even an inkling of the fact that they would be the cynosure of all eyes that night then she would have stayed home and read a book! It seemed to take forever till they finally reached the far side of the room, and Genevieve accepted the glass of wine Ross brought her from the bar with a sigh of relief. She took a long sip of the pale cool liquid, feeling it inch its way down her throat.

'Better?'

'A bit. Honestly, Ross, I just never imagined that it would be like this. I supposed I hadn't fully appreciated just how interested people are in you and your affairs.'

She stared up at him, her eyes faintly troubled as the full realisation of what she'd let herself in for finally hit home. 'I don't know if I'm going to be able to cope with it. I'm not used to being the centre of attention.'

'You'll manage, Genevieve. You have to. H.R. Holdings is just too important to worry about a few ruffled feelings.'

'A few. . .now look here. . .'

'Well, well—Ross and the lovely Miss Gray! What a surprise!'

Genevieve recognised the voice even before she saw its owner, and a chill of cold anticipation shivered through her. She pinned a falsely bright smile to her lips and turned, unconsciously moving closer to Ross for support.

'Mr Jameson. Good evening.'

Henry Jameson was one of the members of the board whom Genevieve disliked most of all, the really rotten apple in the whole miserable barrel. His hostility towards her at that first board meeting, and in several of the comments he had made to the papers, had made her dislike him from the outset. Approaching fifty, a small, rather corpulent man with cold grey eyes behind silver-framed glasses, he was a power to be contended with at H.R. Holdings. From what she'd learned in the past few days, he had been the main instigator behind the recent attempt to take over the company, and it was obvious that there was little love lost between him and Ross. She could feel the tension almost oozing out of Ross as he faced him, and without thinking she slipped her fingers into his, wanting to give as well as seek reassurance.

The gesture wasn't lost on the older man. His face tightened perceptibly and he raised his glass in a cynically mocking toast.

'Here's to the new alliance at H.R., or so it appears. I must say that after your little confrontation the other day at the meeting, this *is* a surprise. Can it be real, I ask myself?'

'Oh, it's real enough, Henry. Don't be put off by the way we acted the other day; that was business, nothing personal. Still, there are compensations for falling out like that, aren't there, darling?' Ross bent his head, pressing his lips to Genevieve's in a swift tender kiss that left her reeling and unable to do anything but nod her agreement. 'Genevieve and I knew each other way before we learned of the bequest, you know, and this has only served to bring us closer together.'

'Fancy! Now I wonder how the bloodhounds of the Press managed to miss that? I thought they were permanently following your scent, Ross. After all, you usually manage to throw them a juicy story or two about your conquests.'

There was an insulting note in the man's voice, but Ross ignored it with a panache Genevieve envied. Throwing back his dark head, he laughed.

'There are ways and means, Henry, especially if it's important to you. Those stories provided, how shall I put it. . .a nice smokescreen for something far more important.'

'Oh, come on, Ross! Just tell me where in this whole town you two could meet and yet not be recognised?'

'My house. You've not seen it yet, have you, Henry? Way off the beaten track, it is. Of course, it still needs a lot of work doing to it, but it will be the perfect family home in a few months' time. Genevieve and I have spent a lot of time deciding exactly what should be done there.'

Genevieve's mouth fell open a fraction and she snapped it shut, terrified that the perceptive Henry would understand what had caused such a reaction. She raised her glass and took a gulp of the wine, almost choking as Henry spoke again.

'That sounds almost as if some sort of permanent arrangement is being planned. Can we expect an

announcement in the near future, then, Ross?'
Henry's eyes focused on Ross in a piercing stare, but
he met it levelly.

'Oh, I think you'll have to wait and see about
that, Henry. I wouldn't want to give any secrets
away just yet.'

'No, of course not. Still, it is a thought, isn't it?
Not just a marriage, so to speak, but a merging of
shares and business interests. It would make your
position as head of H.R. guaranteed.'

'Oh, but. . .' About to delcare that any thought
of marriage between her and Ross Harper would
only succeed in doing the exact opposite by splitting
up the shares, Genevieve fell silent as Ross tightened
his grip on her hand, his fingers pinching into her
flesh.

'We shall worry about that when and if it happens.
Let's not frighten the lady away with such ideas.
After all, it's Genevieve I'm interested in, not her
shares. Now, if you'll excuse us, Henry, there are a
couple of people I want to introduce Genevieve to
before we go in to dinner.'

'Of course. Don't let me keep you. Oh, by the
way, Ross, I'm having a house party down at my
place in a couple of weeks and I'd be delighted if
you could both come.'

'Love to, wouldn't we, darling? Thanks, Henry.
Enjoy yourself. I'll probably catch you later.'

Ross led Genevieve away, his hand still ruthlessly
clamped round hers, and Genevieve fought down
the desire to wrench herself free till they were safely
out of sight of the older man and tucked in a quiet
corner. With a quick little flick she pulled her hand

out of Ross's grasp, her eyes angry as she rubbed her fingers.

'Do you have to be so rough? And what did you mean back there? You know very well that any hint of us marrying means that the shares will have to be sold. Why did you lead him on like that?'

'I know the terms of the will and so do you, but no one else does. They weren't made public. As far as I'm concerned, the more people who think our relationship is permanent the better.'

'I suppose I can understand that, but why didn't you tell me? I could have ruined everything just now with one careless word.'

'I know. I'm sorry.' Ross ran his hand through his hair, ruffling the dark strands till they lay in rakish disarray across his forehead, and Genevieve had to clamp down on the sudden crazy urge that rose inside her to reach up and smooth them back into place.

'Look, Genevieve, this whole thing has been like a bolt from the blue. Coming on top of all the recent attempts to take over the company, it's been very hard to come to terms with. Frankly, the thought of H.R.'s falling into outsiders' hands haunts me so that I can think of little else, even passing on campaign plans to my partner. So forgive me. . .please?'

He smiled at her, his eyes gentle, his face holding a hint of weariness that made a surge of tenderness well up inside her. She smiled gently back at him, knowing she couldn't add to the strain he was obviously working under.

'Of course I will.'

'Thank you. I'd hate you to think that I'm trying

to use you when you've been so reasonable about it all. I just genuinely forgot to tell you.' He took her hand again, twining his long cool fingers through her slender ones, linking them together. 'Now come along, partner. There's plenty more of the enemy out there to rout. Forward into battle!'

Genevieve laughed and clung to his hand, letting him lead her back into the noisy bustle of the room. Just for a second a tiny alarm bell rang inside her, the first small warning signal, but with a toss of her head she cut it off dead. She wanted to help Ross Harper all she could, wanted to hear that warmth for her in his voice again and again and again. She would worry about the sense of it later.

The air was cool and soft, playing gently over her hot flushed skin, clearing the stuffy fog from her head. Genevieve drew her shawl round her shoulders and lifted her face to the breeze, winnowing the silky hair away from her hot neck as she revelled in the cool touch of the night air. Behind her the strains of the orchestra filtered from the ballroom, playing a gentle waltz, and she hummed softly to herself, her slender body swaying to the rhythm.

'So here you are. I wondered where you'd got to.'

Ross stepped through the tall french doors, pulling them closed behind him as he came to join her on the terrace. Genevieve smiled at him, watching the way the dim soft light spilling from the ballroom played over his face. He really was the most handsome man she had ever seen. With a tiny sigh of regret she looked away, knowing that line of thought was dangerous.

'It was so hot in there I couldn't stand it a moment longer. I thought I'd come out and get a breath of air. Aren't the gardens lovely?'

'Mmm, lovely.' There was a note in his deep voice which made Genevieve look quickly at him, and she felt the colour race to her cheeks as she saw that he wasn't looking at the night-darkened gardens but directly at her! He smiled, his face gently teasing, and she dropped her eyes, feeling suddenly breathless and shaken. Despite the attention, the scrutiny from the other guests, the evening had been marvellous, and Genevieve knew that she would remember every second of it. Maybe it *had* just been for show, to convince their interested audience of their relationship, but Ross had gone out of his way to be charming to her, paying her little compliments, giving her all his attention. A girl could get used to being treated like that, as though she was someone very special, very used indeed!

'Tired?'

Leaning back against the stone balcony rail, Ross stared down at her, and Genevieve moved slightly, feeling far too aware of him and his closeness for comfort.

'A—a little, but it's been a lovely night, better than I thought it would be when we arrived,' she said with a wry little grimace.

Ross laughed, his teeth gleaming startlingly white against his tanned skin in the dim soft light. 'The look on your face when we were announced, Genevieve—it was terrific! I've seen rabbits looking less scared than that!'

Genevieve chuckled, unable to take offence at such gentle teasing. 'Well, it's all right for you. You're used to lots of media attention, so this was probably nothing to you, having to face all those gawking people, but it's rather different for me. I've never been a celebrity before.'

'I know, and I really am grateful, Genevieve. I can't tell you how much I appreciate what you've done tonight. I just wish. . .'

The french doors were suddenly flung open and a group of people spilled out on to the terrace, their noisy laughter cutting through the intimate silence. With a wry look, Ross took her hand and pulled her towards the shallow flight of steps leading down to the lawn. 'Let's get out of here, shall we? Something tells me things are going to get a little wild in a moment or two.'

Genevieve went willingly with him, not anxious to hurry back inside the crowded, stuffy ballroom. As they moved further away from the building, the night's velvety softness closed round them and the sounds of laughter and revelry became muted murmurs. The high heels of her sandals sank in the soft spongy grass and she stopped, holding on to Ross's arm as she slipped them off and looped them over her fingers, feeling the delicious coolness of the earth beneath her feet.

Ross looked down at her and smiled, a faint tenderness in his expression. 'I never realised you were so small before.'

'Small? I'm not small,' she said indignantly, glaring back at him. 'I'm five feet five!'

'Oh, my. . .so big!'

With a low chuckle he pulled her against him, looping his arm easily round her slender waist as he fitted her against his side so close that with every step she could feel the hard brush of his thigh against hers. She gulped, all the indignation wiped away in the face of far deeper, shocking feelings. She held herself rigid, knowing she should pull away from the disturbing touch of his body against hers, yet some sort of inner demon wouldn't let her.

All right, so the only reason that they were here, like this, walking in the moonlight, was because she had rashly agreed to help him. But would it really matter if for a few minutes she let herself pretend that Ross was here because he wanted to be, because he really and truly had wanted to be her escort for the evening? The night was far too magical to let the harshness of reality spoil it completely.

Silently, their steps in harmony, they walked down the length of the sweeping shadowed lawns, stopping only when they came to the river. Ross leant back against the massive trunk of a trailing willow tree, pulling Genevieve against him so that her shoulders rested against the broad, muscled hardness of his chest.

For a few quiet minutes they stared out across the water, watching the silvered rays of moonlight bounce off the gentle ripples. Then slowly, gently Ross turned her round, his eyes intent as he stared down into her upturned face.

Genevieve's pulse leapt and missed a beat before racing wildly, sending the blood pounding and rippling through her veins like exploding bubbles of champagne. He was so close that she could see the

tiny pale lines fanned round his blue eyes, could feel
the warm, moist brush of his breath against her hair,
could smell the faint tangy smell of spicy cologne
that clung to his skin. A thousand danger signals
were springing to life inside her, flashing red, clang-
ing wildly, yet it was hard to heed a single one of
them. She was drowning in sensation, in the feel of
him, the closeness, the intimacy of the moment, but
somehow she just had to be sensible.

'Ross, I don't think. . .'

'Shhh! Don't think, Genevieve,' he whispered.
'Don't think at all. Just feel.'

He bent his head and Genevieve knew that he was
going to kiss her, yet she didn't move, didn't try to
turn her head away. Suddenly, shockingly, she
wanted this kiss, wanted it with an intensity which
was almost frightening.

Softly, gently, his lips brushed over hers, teasing,
tasting, the faint tantalising pressure making her
ache for something more, some deeper sort of
caress. Reaching up on tiptoe, she wound her arms
round his neck, pulling his mouth more firmly down
to hers, feeling the shudder that rippled through his
body with a hot flare of triumph.

With a speed that left her breathless, he parted
her lips and deepened the kiss, his tongue plunging
into the dark sweet recesses of her mouth to mate
with hers. Genevieve clung to him as wave after
wave of wild sensation flooded through her, leaving
her weak and shaken. All around them the night
was cool, quiet, still, but there was nothing cool
about the feel of their bodies pressed close together,

nothing quiet about the hot rush of blood through their veins, nothing still about the heavy noisy pounding of their hearts.

His hands slid down her back, moulding her body against him, pressing her closer and closer, and Genevieve felt something primitive spring to life inside her as she felt the unmistakable hardness of him against her softness. Liquid fire raced through the pit of her stomach, making her ache for something she had never known, some release from this delicious torment. Unconsciously, she pressed herself closer and heard Ross gasp, a harsh rasp of sound as though he was fighting for his very last breath. Then slowly he raised his head, his hands trembling as they traced lightly up and down the delicate bones of her spine through the thin silk of her dress, bringing her gently back from that wild crazy moment they had just shared, bringing her back to reality.

Genevieve pulled away, feeling the cool air flood over her heated skin, and shivered. She wrapped her arms tightly round her body and turned away to stare out over the river, desperately needing a few seconds to re-gather her composure. If anyone had suggested that she would respond to a man, any man, like that, with that sort of abandon, then she would have laughed. Now the laughter would hold a very hollow ring. Ross Harper had stirred her senses, had indeed stirred senses she hadn't even known she possessed, but it had to stop. There was no way she could continue with their agreement on this basis. She didn't have the strength to do that.

She swung round, her face pale but set with a quiet determination.

'Ross. . .'

'Genevieve. . .'

Both spoke together, then stopped abruptly, staring at each other. Ross straightened, pushing himself away from the tree-trunk, his face strangely bleak as he stared down at her.

'I know what you're going to say,' he said quietly, 'and I'm sorry, Genevieve. That was never planned. Blame it on the moonlight, the wine, or whatever, but rest assured that it won't happen again. I'm just as anxious as you to avoid any kind of personal entanglement. Our arrangement is purely business, nothing else. Agreed?'

Genevieve nodded, then bent down to refasten the thin straps of her sandals while she hid the shimmer of tears which had sprung to her eyes. He was right, of course, and she had been about to say much the same thing to him, so why did she feel this horrible sense of loss, this wrenching ache of pain? There was nothing between her and Ross Harper other than a business arrangement. Anything else was only foolish dreams and crazy longings. H.R. Holdings was all he loved: there could be no place in his heart for her even if she'd been mad enough to want there to be. The thought was oddly depressing.

In silence they made their way back through the gardens, and Genevieve pulled the wispy shawl tightly round her shoulders, feeling chilled to the bone. Before, the cool night breeze had felt delicious flowing over her skin, but now it felt like a cruel flood of icy water. Those few minutes in Ross's arms had been magical, but now the spell was broken and all that was left was a strange feeling of loss, a sense of sorrow.

Ross slid his hand under her elbow as they mounted the steps to cross the terrace and go in through the french doors, but Genevieve halted, her face mirroring her reluctance to rejoin the other guests. She glanced round, not quite able to meet Ross's eyes, terrified that he would read far more in her expression at this moment than she was prepared to let him. 'Would you mind if we left now? I'm rather tired and don't feel like going back into that fray again.'

'Of course. I must admit that I've had enough for one night too.'

There was a strange note in his deep voice and Genevieve shot him a swift look, wondering exactly what had caused it. Was he bored with her, tired of having to pretend an interest in a woman he would never have asked out in different circumstances? Had it all been such a trial to him, then, even that kiss?

Anger and a large measure of hurt speared through her at the thought and she pulled away abruptly, her slender body tense.

'What's the matter?' Ross stared at her curiously, his blue eyes sweeping over the faint flush that edged her cheekbones, the mutinous set to her softly curved chin. 'Genevieve?'

'Nothing,' she said coldly. 'Absolutely nothing at all. So let's go, shall we?'

Holding herself rigid, she walked ahead of him, keeping a cool little smile pinned to her lips as she said goodbye to several people she'd been introduced to. On the outside she appeared composed, yet inside she was a mass of torment and self-recriminations. How could she have been so foolish as to believe, even for a second, that Ross actually liked her and enjoyed her company? It had all been an act, a deliberate attempt to convince onlookers that their relationship was real. Well, quite frankly, he deserved an Oscar for his performance tonight. It had been so good that she had almost believed it herself!

There was a queue of departing guests lined up in the hallway and Genevieve stood tapping her foot with impatience as she waited their turn to leave. She could feel Ross watching her, but she refused to look at him, refused to let him see just how angry and how hurt she felt. The worst thing was that she only had herself to blame. She had known the score right from the beginning, so why had she let him kiss her like that and kissed him back with such wild abandon? Soft lights, sweet music and a little wine had never had that sort of effect before!

It seemed to take forever before they reached the doorway, and Genevieve grimaced as she realised what had caused the hold-up. A group of photographers had positioned themselves on the steps and were taking photographs of the guests as they left. There was a distinct look of boredom on their faces, a look that changed to avid interest the minute Ross appeared. En masse they surged forward, and Genevieve blinked at the blinding glare of a dozen flashbulbs. For a crazy moment she understood exactly how a lion-tamer must feel when he entered the cage, but at least he had a whip and chair to keep the beasts at bay. She had absolutely nothing!

Instinctively, she stepped back a pace, stopping as she cannoned into Ross, who was right behind her. He took her arm, his touch light yet strangely steadying.

'How about telling us who the lovely lady is, Mr Harper?' one of the photographers shouted from the group, and Ross laughed easily, grinning round at them.

'Don't you know, fellas? You must be slipping! Still, it is late, I suppose, so maybe I can understand your ignorance. This, gentlemen, is Miss Genevieve Gray.'

There was a sudden murmur, then a scrabble for notebooks as the waiting journalists scented a story and began to write furiously. An older man at the back stepped forward, his eyes gleaming with speculation as he looked at Ross and Genevieve standing so close together.

'And is it true that you and Miss Gray are contemplating some other sort of alliance apart from business? Matrimony, for instance?'

There was a sudden silence, broken only by the soft sound of pencils racing over paper. Genevieve bit back a groan as she realised exactly what was going to be in the morning papers. How had he got hold of that story? Who had given it to him? Simple questions with an equally simple answer—Henry Jameson! She had seen him a little ahead of them in the queue. It was more than likely that he had given the reporter that snippet of information.

She glanced at Ross, her eyes dark with concern,

but he smiled calmly back at her, his fingers tightening fractionally in a silent warning she scarcely needed. If he thought she was going to spill her innermost thoughts and feelings to this pack of scandalmongers, then he must think she was really green!

'No comment, gentlemen,' he said quietly, leading her forward.

'Oh, come on! Not that old line. Our readers want something better than that.'

'And I don't doubt that they'll get it, but it's as much as I'm prepared to say. So if you'll excuse us, we'll be on our way home.'

'Whose home. . .yours or hers?'

There was a chuckle of laughter from the group at the witticism, and Genevieve felt her face flame with colour. She looked down, keeping her face averted from the interested, speculative stares as Ross steered her away towards the car. He didn't say anything till they were out of earshot of the reporters.

'I'm sorry they embarrassed you back there, Genevieve. They didn't really mean any harm. It's just their way.' There was genuine concern in his voice as he studied her hectically flushed face, and she summoned up a shaky smile, wishing she could handle remarks like that with much more poise and sophistication.

'I know. It's just their job, I suppose, and of course it's what we came here tonight for, isn't it? To give the public the impression that you and I are. . .' Her throat closed on the word and she fell silent, staring up at him, her eyes huge and shadowed.

Ross stopped, pulling her gently round in front of him to hold her by the shoulders.

'Lovers, Genevieve,' he said softly. 'And it isn't such a terrible thing in this day and age, is it?'

'I. . .I suppose not,' she whispered back shakily. 'It's just me. I'm rather old-fashioned about these things, I guess.' She forced a thin smile to her lips, but it didn't seem to fool him for a second. There was no way she could be blasé about such an idea, no way at all, and it showed.

'Have you never had a lover, then, Genevieve?' he asked, a touch of incredulity showing briefly on his face.

'No.' Her voice was low, the barest thread of sound against a background noise of laughter and car doors slamming. There were dozens of people about, walking down the drive, calling and shouting to each other as they collected their cars, yet somehow it felt as though she and Ross were completely alone, separated from the rest of the world on their own little island. The air between them seemed to be humming with tension, with unspoken words and feelings. She knew she should pull away, should stop this ridiculously intimate conversation now, yet the look in his eyes, the touch of his hands, held her spellbound.

'Why not?'

She shrugged, dropping her eyes to study the shadows gathered like puddles of ink across the tree-lined driveway. 'I don't know, really. It's just never seemed right. I—I've never wanted anyone like that.' She laughed, a brittle little sound. 'Perhaps I'm one of those women you read about in all those glossy magazines—you know, frigid.'

Ross chuckled, his deep voice filled with a wicked amusement and a hint of intimacy that made her blood quicken. 'Oh, no, Genevieve, you're far from that, believe me. I think I can vouch for that fact after tonight. No woman who can kiss like that, with such passion, can ever be classed as frigid!'

Genevieve closed her eyes, wishing the ground would open up and swallow her. She pulled away from his grasp and hurried towards the car, waiting silently while he unlocked the door for her. She bent to slip inside, stopping abruptly as he caught her hand to stop her.

In the dim moonlight his face was mainly shadowed, the sharp angles softened. Only his eyes seemed vividly alive as they glittered down at her. Lifting his hand, he ran his thumb gently over the soft curve of her lips, the light pressure so tantalising, so evocative, that she gasped.

'There's nothing to be ashamed of in wanting someone, Genevieve. It's as natural as breathing.'

'Maybe,' she answered, her voice husky with emotion. 'But sex to me is something special, the result of love, of sharing, of commitment. It's not something to be grabbed at, like a handful of sweets. When I take a lover, Ross, it will be for one reason only: because I love him and want to give myself to him in the most intimate way possible.'

'Few people share that view nowadays, Genevieve. Very few women especially. I have the impression that a lot of women see sex as a bargaining factor, a chance to get what they can from a man.'

Genevieve pulled away and shivered, her whole body going cold at the thought of doing that. When she spoke her voice was clear, filled with conviction.

'I'm afraid I don't agree with you on that score, Ross. Maybe some women do see it in that light; I don't know. All I can say is that it's not my view at all. Perhaps you've been unfortunate in meeting the wrong sort of women.'

He stared at her in silence for a moment, his eyes tracing over her face, searching her features as though looking for an answer to something that eluded him. Then he smiled, the edge of tension easing swiftly from him. 'Then perhaps it's a good job that Grandfather left you those shares after all, Genevieve.'

'What do you mean?' Startled, she stared up at him, feeling her pulse race at the expression in his eyes, the gentleness, the teasing, tender hint of laughter.

'That perhaps you can set me right about what to look for in a woman, set me on the right path so that I don't make so many mistakes in the future.'

'I doubt if there's anything I can teach you about love and romance, Ross Harper,' she said shortly. 'You could write a textbook on it by now, with your experience!'

'Think so? Well, you could be right.' He slammed the car door and walked round to the driver's side, starting the engine with a little roar before turning to look at her. 'But even experts need a bit of help now and then, you know. We're only human.'

He set the car into gear and pulled away, while Genevieve sat back in her seat, feeling more shaken by that silly little conversation than she should have. Only human—well, he was that all right, and so was she, and *that* was where the trouble really lay!

CHAPTER EIGHT

GENEVIEVE folded the green silk scarf into a neat square, then tucked it down into the corner of the suitcase. She glanced round the room, then picked up the list, and skimmed through it, mentally ticking off each item to check that she'd not forgotten anything. No, that was it, as far as she could tell. She shouldn't need anything more for the weekend stay at Henry Jameson's country house, except, perhaps, for a bottle of tranquillisers: just the thought of the coming two days was giving her the jitters!

With a sigh she closed the lid of the case and carried it through to the sitting-room, resting it against the end of the sofa where she'd left her handbag. She looked round, wondering what little task she could find to fill in the next hour till Ross collected her but, frankly, she'd done everything which needed to be done, even down to watering the pot plants.

Too restless and on edge to sit, she prowled round the flat, straightening a cushion here, smoothing a cover there, aware that her stomach felt like a refugee from a roller-coaster ride. Maybe a cup of strong coffee would help settle her nerves and give her the boost needed to face the coming ordeal, though why she had ever let that wretched man talk her into such an act of folly was beyond her. Two days and three nights in Ross Harper's company, and under Henry Jameson's scrutiny, was the stuff of nightmares!

Gritting her teeth against the mounting wave of hysteria, Genevieve hurried through to the kitchen and filled the kettle. She leant back against the worktop while she waited for it to boil, her mind drifting back over the past few weeks, drifting back to Ross, as it seemed to do time and again each day.

She must have been out with him a dozen times now: intimate little dinners in expensive restaurants, exclusive lunches, glitzy first nights at the theatre, all the places where they were guaranteed to get maximum Press exposure and be seen by the right people. Ross had been a charming companion on these occasions, keeping conversation to impersonal topics and going out of his way to put her at ease, yet Genevieve knew she still hadn't come to terms with it all, couldn't take it for granted. She was far too aware of Ross, too conscious of him and the effect he'd had on her that night after the ball, to ever do that!

The kettle came to the boil, hissing and spitting steam across the kitchen, and Genevieve brought her mind back to the task at hand and made the drink. She carried it through to the sitting-room and sat down, reaching for a magazine off the pile on the coffee-table and muttering crossly as the whole lot slid to the floor. Bending down to gather them up again, she paused as a photograph in one of them caught her eye. Slowly, almost reluctantly, she smoothed it out, kneeling down on the carpet as she stared at the familiar faces of her and Ross.

The photograph was one of those taken after the Ball and showed them standing close together on the Town Hall steps, with Ross's hands curved lightly round her shoulders. He was smiling down at her, an expression of tenderness on his face which made Genevieve's insides turn to water.

Had he really looked at her like that, or was it just a trick of the light, the angle of the camera? Studying that picture, it wasn't difficult to believe that the accompanying text was right, that there was some sort of romantic commitment between them. How she wished it were true!

The thought shocked her and she straightened abruptly, crumpling the paper into a ball before tossing it into the waste-basket as she should have done days before. She sat back on the sofa and drank the coffee, desperately trying to wipe the thought from her mind, but it was impossible, and after a moment she realised that the only way she could cope with the coming weekend was to face up to what was happening to her.

She was attracted to Ross Harper. For weeks now she had fought against the idea, but there was no way she could fight it any longer. She scarcely knew him, yet something inside her responded to him with a wild sort of abandon. Somehow, though, she had to remember that they were both playing parts, that, no matter how real it all appeared, it was just an act, a way to safeguard H.R. Holdings. To allow herself to be caught up in the spell he exerted was courting trouble, because when all this was over, and the company was once more safely under his control, then he would forget about her. Her only comfort then would be to know that she hadn't made a complete and utter fool of herself. It seemed a very cold sort of comfort indeed.

Two hours later Genevieve was still sitting on the sofa, seething with anger as she drank her third cup of coffee. Where on earth was Ross? What did he mean by leaving her waiting here like this? Did he think he was the only busy person in the whole wide world and that she had nothing better to do than sit here twiddling her thumbs and cooling her heels till he chose to make an appearance? She could have spent all these wasted hours at the shop, catching up on some of the backlog of paperwork. If the business folded then she would hold him personally responsible!

The telephone rang, and she slammed the cup down and leapt to answer it. If it was Ross then she was really going to give him a piece of her. . .

'Genevieve?'

The familiar voice coming so clearly over the line made her go suddenly weak and shaky. She clutched hold of the receiver, desperately trying to whip her anger up again, but it seemed impossible at that moment. Why had she never realised before just how deliciously deep and sexy his voice was, and just what sort of an effect it could have on a poor susceptible female?

'Are you still there? Damn it, Genevieve, I'm in a hurry, so stop playing games and answer me!'

The snap of anger in his voice cut through the momentary weakness and whipped her back to her senses. She stood up straighter, her voice frosted with ice as she answered coldly, 'Yes, sir! And what did you want, sir?'

There was a brief pause, then Ross laughed softly. 'Sorry, I didn't mean to sound as though I was issuing orders. Just habit, I expect. Listen, something urgent has come up and I'm stuck in a meeting. It's going to be some time till I can get away, so I think it would be better if you made your own way to Henry's.'

'Well, I'm not sure if I can. . .' Genevieve trailed off, a feeling of reluctance welling inside her. Facing Henry Jameson with Ross as back-up was one thing, facing him on her own was something else entirely! 'Just how long will you be, Ross? I mean, wouldn't it be better if I meet you there, wherever you are, then we can go together. I don't know if I can handle that man's brand of "charm" all by myself.'

Ross chuckled. 'Genevieve, you could handle anything! I have every confidence in you. I'm still in Birmingham at present, so there's no point in your coming to meet me. It's a good hour or more's drive up the motorway. It would be far easier if I could go straight to Henry's without having to make a detour back into town to collect you. I wouldn't ask, but this weekend is important, far more so than I imagined it would be. One of our major investors in the new precinct has been invited as well, and I want to be there just to keep an eye on what Henry is up to. I don't trust that man; he's after control of the company, but I'll see him in hell before I let that happen!'

There was a grimness in his voice, and Genevieve shivered as she heard it. That Ross Harper would make a bad enemy she didn't doubt. She could only be grateful that at present he regarded her as an ally.

'Well, I suppose I'll have to agree if you think it's for the best, but I don't want to arrive too early. You may be confident that I can handle things, but I'm afraid I don't share that feeling. What time do you think you'll get there?'

'Any time before midnight is the best I can say. I'll leave it up to you what time you decide on and phone Henry to warn him we'll both be late.'

'Fine. I'll see you later, then.'

'Yes. . .and, Genevieve?'

'What?'

'Take care.'

The line went dead and slowly Genevieve replaced the receiver, her hand lingering on it for a second, clinging hold of the fragile link with Ross a while longer. 'Take care'. . .a casual, everyday sort of statement, yet it warmed her that he should care enough to make it. Was it possible that Ross did feel something more for her than he would feel for a mere business partner, that he was becoming interested in her as a woman?

For a long, delirious minute, Genevieve hugged the hope to her, feeling warmth steal through her body, then, slowly, the warmth faded, paled before the cold truth of the situation. No matter what happened or how Ross felt he would never do anything to jeopardise the company. The terms of his grandfather's will might have brought them together, yet they would be instrumental in keeping them apart. What had been in the old man's mind

when he had made such a bequest, on the one hand
giving so much yet on the other taking even more?
Genevieve didn't know and doubted if she ever
would. All she knew with a cold chilling certainty
was that any hopes of a relationship between her
and Ross were pipe dreams. They would disappear
like smoke the moment they were confronted by the
possible loss of H.R. Holdings.

She left the flat at eight o'clock, stopping at the
petrol station to fill the old van's tank before heading
out of town to join the twisting network of back
roads. Traffic was light, with just a few drivers taking
advantage of the fine weather, so that Genevieve
was able to relax, driving automatically while her
mind wandered. The sudden sharp explosion as the
back tyre burst, followed by the van slewing sideways, took her completely by surprise.

Wrenching on the steering wheel, she managed to
pull the van on to the grass verge and jumped down
from the cab. She hurried round to the back, her
heart sinking as she took swift stock of the strands
of rubber fanning out from what was left of the back
tyre. Heaven alone knew what had caused such a
blow-out, but it was lucky that she had been travel-
ling slowly down a quiet road and not down the
motorway. It could have caused a very nasty accident indeed.

With a sigh of annoyance, she stripped off her
pale blue linen jacket and opened the back doors to
get the spare wheel, her eyes widening in dismay
when she located it and saw that it was as flat as a
pancake. Why hadn't she bothered to check it regu-
larly? Now what was she going to do?

With a cold feeling in the pit of her stomach Genevieve climbed down again and stared along the road, wondering how much further she had to go, but there was no clue to be had from the never-ending ribbon of grey tarmac and green hedgerows. She could be one mile or ten away from her destination, and thanks to her daydreaming she had no way of knowing which it was. So should she stand here, helplessly waiting for the cavalry to come and rescue her, or should she set off walking to the nearest village and find a phone? Somehow she had the feeling that the cavalry might be unavailable this evening!

She retrieved her jacket and slipped it on again before picking up the suitcase, somehow loath to leave it behind and arrive at Henry Jameson's without a change of clothing. She locked the van, then set off, keeping to the grass verge to avoid any passing cars, though there was little traffic on the road now. A few cars passed her, but she didn't try to attract the drivers' attention. There was no way she wanted to find herself in even more trouble than she was in already by accepting a lift from a stranger.

Gradually the warm summer evening began to darken, the sky turning to a deep purplish-red, casting long shadows across the road. For the umpteenth time Genevieve swapped the case from one hand to the other, wondering why it felt as though it was filled with lead rather than a few silky undergarments and cotton dresses. Her fingers were cramped, her shoulders aching, her feet blistered from walking in thin strappy sandals more suited to town pavements than route-marching. All in all, she had never felt more miserable in the whole of her life, and she knew exactly who to blame for her discomfort: Ross Harper! Damn him. If he hadn't been so engrossed in his meeting then none of this would ever have happened.

Tears of self-pity and tiredness sprang to her eyes and she put the case down to wipe them away. For a minute she allowed herself the sheer luxury of relaxing, letting every single strained and aching muscle collapse into a quivering little heap before determinedly rallying herself again. There was no point in standing here bemoaning the situation when it would change nothing. She had to press on.

She took a firm grip on the suitcase handle once again, flexing her stiff fingers before heaving it off the ground with a shade more enthusiasm than was strictly necessary. She staggered sideways, yelping in sudden pain as a thick bramble hidden in the long grass snaked round her ankle, biting deep into the tender flesh. Dropping the case, she bent down to work it free, her heart leaping in alarm as a car roared round the bend in the road, missing her by mere inches. With a squeal of brakes and a slither of gravel, it ground to a halt a few yards in front of her.

Trapped by the bramble, Genevieve could only stand and stare at the man who climbed out and strode towards her, her eyes widening in astonishment.

'Ross! But I never expected to. . .'

'What the hell do you think you're playing at, woman?'

No hello, no how nice to see you or can I help

you; just that single furious question, which was the final straw after all she'd gone through.

'Why, having a picnic, of course. Don't you think this is just the perfect place for it?' Cold sarcasm dripped from the words, but Ross ignored it, his dark brows drawing together in anger.

'You can cut out the smart answers, lady, if you know what's good for you,' he snapped, taking a step towards her. 'What's going on? Haven't you got more sense than to go wandering round lonely country lanes at this time of night? Anyone could have come along and. . .'

His voice trailed off, as though he couldn't quite bring himself to voice the possibilities. Genevieve shot him a startled look, something about the stern expression on his face, the rigidity of his tall body, making her temper her words with caution. Frankly, right at that moment Ross Harper looked dangerous, ready to explode, and there was no way she was going to put a light to the fuse.

'I had a blow-out in the van and as the spare tyre was flat, I decided I'd better try to walk and phone for help.'

'Walk? On your own at this time of night? Anything could have happened!'

For a second his eyes burned down into hers, filled with anger and something else, a real live fear. Then with a low groan he pulled her to him, holding her close while he rested his forehead against hers, and with a start of surprise Genevieve felt the trembling spasm that shook him.

Had he really been so afraid for her safety, then? Had that been the reason for his unreasonable anger? The thought held her spellbound, so that she didn't try to pull away from his hold.

'When I spotted your van back there, with the tyre ripped and the wheel buckled, and no sign of you, I nearly went frantic!'

'Did you? I'm sorry, Ross, but what else could I do? I couldn't sit there all night in the hope that someone might come along and rescue me, now could I? Don't be angry with me.' She glanced up at him from under the silky sweep of her long lashes, watching the way his lips tightened into a thin straight line. 'Please!'

'Genevieve, I'm not angry with *you*, can't you see that? I'm angry with myself!'

'With your. . .what on earth do you mean?' She pulled back a fraction, trying to ease a bit of space between them so she could study his face, but Ross wouldn't let her go. Linking his hands behind her waist, he held her close, the firm hard strength of his thighs pressing against her.

'Simply that none of this would ever have happened if I'd collected you as arranged. It's all my fault, and if something had happened to you then I would never have forgiven myself.'

'But it didn't, did it?' she asked logically, forgetting her own previous annoyance in the face of his obvious distress. 'Look, Ross, I'm a grown woman, I can't expect to have anyone dancing attendance on me just in case things go wrong. I should have checked on the spare wheel before I set out, not waited till I had a puncture to find it was flat too. And when all's said and done, the worst I've suffered is a couple of nasty blisters and a few scratches from

this bramble, nothing else. I'm still all in one piece.'
She smiled up at him, her eyes gleaming a soft gold
in the pale moonlight, and felt her pulse leap as he
slowly drew her even closer.

'Yes,' he said softly, staring down into her
upturned face. 'All in one piece, and such a beautiful
little piece too.'

He bent his head, and Genevieve tensed. Was he
going to kiss her, after all he'd said the other night?
Fire raced through her as she waited for the touch
of his lips on hers, followed by an aching flare of
disappointment as he did no more than brush a light
kiss over the smooth sweep of her brow.

He stepped back, his hands falling to his sides, his
face unreadable as he stared silently at her for a
long, timeless moment. Genevieve drew in a slow,
deep breath, bending down to untwine the last
clinging strands of vine from her ankle while she hid
her expression from his too discerning gaze. He *had*
been going to kiss her, she just knew it. So what had
suddenly made him change his mind that way?

'It wouldn't work, Genevieve. We both know
that.'

His voice was soft, like deep velvet, warm, entic-
ing, and she shivered, hating her own helpless reaction to it, the sudden flare of longing.

'I don't know what you mean, Ross,' she said,
straightening. She forced herself to meet his eyes
levelly and deny every single emotion clamouring
inside her. 'Now don't you think we'd better be
going? Henry will think we've chickened out because
we've something to hide, and that will never do!'

She reached out for the case, snatching her hand

back as her fingers brushed unexpectedly against his. Helplessly, she stared at him, unable to hide her reaction to the brief contact, and heard him swear under his breath.

'Don't, Genevieve,' he said harshly. 'Don't look at me like that, or God knows I'll do something both you and I will regret. Our arrangement is purely business. We can't allow any personal feelings to come into it, or. . .'

'Or what, Ross?' she questioned softly, studying the strain etched on his face.

'Or nothing,' he said abruptly.

He swung round, tossing the case into the back of the car with a barely veiled violence, and Genevieve watched him, feeling shaken to the very depths of her soul by the unexpected exchange. Just hours ago she had finally faced the fact that she was attracted to this man, yet not once had she allowed for the possibility that he might feel the same way about her! The very idea filled her with fear. . .and a crazy wild elation!

CHAPTER NINE

SUNLIGHT poured hotly over her body, warming her skin, making her feel deliciously lethargic, and Genevieve closed her eyes. In the distance she could hear the faint steady thud of a ball as Ross and Philippe Gérard, another of Henry's house guests, played tennis, but she was far too sleepy to pay much attention to it. Who in their right mind would want to play tennis on such a glorious day, with the temperature pushing well into the eighties? Not her. She was content to lounge here by the side of the pool and nap.

Easing down on to the padded lounger, she let her mind drift pleasantly over the past few hours, somewhat surprised to find that she was enjoying herself. True, Henry had been his usual prickly self, and she still had the feeling that she was tiptoeing on eggshells around him, but she'd been prepared for that. The other guests had turned out to be a pleasant middle-aged couple who made undemanding conversation and Philippe Gérard, the investor in the new precinct whom Ross had mentioned.

A charmingly urbane Frenchman in his mid-forties, he had made no secret of the fact that he found Genevieve attractive. That she was also bilingual, thanks to her mother, and could converse with him in his native tongue, was an added bonus. He had monopolised her attention at breakfast, and it was

only when she had seen the speculative looks Henry
was giving them and the grimness on Ross's handsome face that she had realised just how her friendli-
ness might be misconstrued.

Caution had made her refuse Philippe's offer of a
game of tennis, claiming that she was far too lazy for
such an energetic form of entertainment. Ross had
accepted, though, with a look in his eyes which
hadn't boded well for the Frenchman's chances, or
for her when it was finished, though for the life of
her she couldn't see what she'd done that was so
wrong. What on earth was the matter with Ross?
Was he just worried that Henry might start having
doubts about their relationship, or was it something
else that had made him glare so coldly at her as he'd
walked off towards the courts?

Suddenly uneasy, she sat up, shading her eyes
against the glare as she stared across the garden
towards the tennis court. The two figures dressed in
white looked tiny from this distance, yet she had no
difficulty in telling which one was Ross. The gleam
of his black hair, the broad set of his shoulders, was
unmistakable.

As she watched, he served, and the ball flew over
the net at top speed. Philippe made a desperate
attempt to reach it before throwing his racket down
in disgust as it sailed past. The two men walked
towards the net and shook hands briefly before
leaving the court and heading back up the garden to
where Genevieve was sitting. Suddenly self-con-
scious about the brevity of her white bikini, she
pulled a thin cotton wrap round her shoulders and
fixed a smile to her lips, hoping that Ross was in a

better temper now he'd won. The weekend would be a strain if he persisted in glaring at her all the time.

'Well, who won?' she asked, politely pretending that she didn't already have a good idea of the score.

Philippe smiled at her, dropping wearily down on to the edge of the lounger, his expression wry.

'Ross, of course, didn't you, *mon ami*? But we shall have the return match tomorrow, I think. Then you will not find me such a pullover.'

'Pushover,' Genevieve corrected automatically, smiling at the tiny lapse in his nearly perfect English. She glanced up at Ross, wanting to share the joke with him, her stomach lurching at the expression on his face. Colour flooded to her cheeks and she looked quickly away, shaken by the coldness in his eyes.

'*Mais oui, ma chérie*, pushover. *Merci*.' Philippe took her hand and pressed a light, half-teasing kiss to it, his black eyes sparkling at her. 'Now I think it is time I changed. Maybe you could swim with me later, Genevieve, *non*?'

'That won't be possible, I'm afraid. Genevieve and I have already arranged to go out this afternoon.' There was little real apology in Ross's voice and Genevieve shot him a startled look, before hurriedly bringing herself under control. What was the matter with him? If he wasn't careful he would end up by antagonising Philippe with his rudeness, and where would that leave H.R. Holdings?

Anxious to smooth things over, she smiled warmly at Philippe. 'Why, yes, I'm afraid that's right. Maybe tomorrow, though, if you still want to.'

Philippe shrugged and stood up, a tiny smile

curving his mouth and making his eyes crinkle as he looked warmly at her.

'Of course. I shall look forward to it. *A bientôt, chérie.*'

Slinging the towel round his neck, he strolled towards the house leaving Genevieve staring after him, her eyes filled with worry. He disappeared through the patio doors and she rounded on Ross, her voice sharp with annoyance.

'What on earth has got into you, Ross? The man's only being friendly. Don't you think you're over-playing your part a bit?'

'We may be playing parts, Genevieve, but it's got to seem real. What do you think Henry's going to believe after this morning's show at the breakfast table? There's no way he's going to believe in our so-called affair if you keep mooning over Gérard like that.'

'Mooning. . .mooning! I've never mooned over anyone in my life, I'll have you know. All I've done is be friendly to him. After all, he is one of your major investors, or have you forgotten that small fact? The way you're going you'll have him pulling out, and then where will you be? You won't find it easy to get a replacement for Philippe and his money at this late stage in the game!' She swung her legs over the side of the lounger and stood up, her body stiff with annoyance at his unjust accusation.

Ross pulled the towel from round his neck and wiped his face, his eyes boring harshly into hers.

'So that's what you call it, is it? Being friendly? Looked more like the old come-on to me. You might be a shareholder, Genevieve, but you don't need to go to those lengths to safeguard your interests!'

'Why, you. . .you. . .!' Incensed by his words and the insult in his tone, she aimed a blow at his cheek, her breath catching sharply as he caught her hand and hauled her roughly against him. For a second his eyes glittered down into hers, filled with anger and something else, something that made her go tense. Electricity arced between them, holding them spellbound, freezing the moment as though the whole world had suddenly ground to a halt.

'Genevieve.' Ross's voice was low, a bare whisper of soft sound mingling gently with the hot stillness of the day, and Genevieve shuddered, feeling as if he had just committed some act of incredible intimacy by saying it that way. She could feel the burning heat of his body, the dampness of his skin where his hand rested against the bare flesh of her waist, and knew she was just one small step away from danger. At that moment she wanted nothing more than to turn her face up to his and kiss him, but she couldn't do that, couldn't take that one small step along a path which could only lead to heartache.

'Genevieve?' he repeated softly, and she looked into his eyes and shook her head.

'No, Ross. No. This has to stop.' She pulled away, turning her face away from him as she stared down the green sweep of garden. 'I. . .I think I'll go in and have a shower before lunch. I'll see you later.'

Legs trembling, she walked up the path and into the house, knowing it was the hardest thing she had ever done to walk away and leave him standing there like that.

They left the house after lunch and headed out of the village, Ross handling the powerful car with a quiet expertise while Genevieve sat silently beside him. She had half expected him to call off their drive after what had happened in the garden, but he was waiting for her when they left the table and she didn't have the heart or the strength to argue with him. Of course he was only going through with it to convince Henry that they wanted some time alone together, yet for the moment she didn't really care. It was enough just to be with him, driving through the warm beauty of the day.

Sitting in the soft leather seat, with the windows wound down and a stream of warm sweet air blowing gently over her flushed face, Genevieve watched him, studying the clean-cut lines of his profile, the way his dark hair curled slightly at the nape of his neck. His hands were strong and steady on the steering wheel, the long fingers guiding the car easily down the narrow winding lanes, and with a tiny shudder Genevieve remembered how it had felt to have those hands on her bare skin.

Sensation rippled through her and she looked away, terrified that Ross might see the naked longing she couldn't hide. Yesterday, just those few short hours ago, she had finally accepted the fact that she was attracted to this man, yet now she knew that attraction had taken a giant step forward. Ross Harper was out of bounds to her; there was a curfew on him as strict and rigid as any that could be imposed, yet nothing could alter the feelings which were suddenly, shockingly springing to life inside her. All she could hope was that, when the time came for them to go their separate ways again, she would find the strength to handle the parting.

Ross turned the car on to a narrow track and drove slowly through a thin copse of trees, stopping on the edge of a small clearing. He cut the engine and leant back in his seat, his face holding a faint grimness as he stared through the windscreen at the sun-dappled patch of brilliant green.

It was obvious that something was troubling him, and just as obvious what that something was. . .her! Ross was worrying what would happen next, if she would allow that recent development in the garden to make her change her mind about their agreement, but he needn't. She had promised to help him in his fight to retain control of the company and she would keep that promise. She wouldn't allow a few moments of wild crazy madness to ruin everything.

She unclipped her seat-belt and turned towards him, her eyes soft as she studied his set face, the tension in his big body.

'Don't worry, Ross,' she said gently. 'Nothing has changed, you know. I'm still going to give Henry a run for his money, or at least, make a good attempt at it. I'm sure we can pull it off.'

Ross smiled faintly, turning to face her, his eyes soft and deep in his tanned face.

'Oh, I'm sure we can, Genevieve, despite what I said earlier. But that isn't the main problem right now.'

'It isn't? But I thought you were worried about the impression we've made, and if I would still keep to my side of the bargain. I will, you know, to the letter. The company is yours, Ross, and I'm determined that nothing is going to change on that score. I appreciate your grandfather's gesture in leaving me those shares, but I still don't know why he did it. I mean, why would he do such a thing, knowing he was jeopardising a company he probably worked long and hard to establish?'

Ross sighed, lifting a hand to run his fingers through his hair. 'Grandfather came to hate the company in the end, Genevieve. He felt that it had ruined my mother's life.'

'How on earth did it do that?' Startled, Genevieve stared at him, seeing the fleeting shadow which crossed his face.

'My mother was the sole heir to Roberts Holdings, a huge concern even thirty years ago. My father, James Harper, was a very ambitious man. He only married her for the company and unfortunately made no bones about the fact afterwards. Grandfather always regretted it, regretted that the company was instrumental in causing her so much unhappiness. He always said that he would make certain it never happened again, that no one else's life would be ruined like that by the lust for money and power. I imagine that's one of the reasons he tied up the shares he left you with so many conditions. He probably thought there was enough of my father's blood in me to run the risk of me marrying you to get them otherwise.'

'And would you have?' The question slipped from her lips before she could stop it, and she felt her cheeks flood with colour as Ross smiled gently at her.

'Who knows? I'm enough of a realist to admit it would be a temptation, and honest enough to say that it wouldn't be any great hardship either. You're a very attractive woman, Genevieve, as I know to my cost.'

'What?' Cheeks flaming, eyes widening, Genevieve stared at him, a frisson of awareness racing through her as he leant forward to run his knuckles gently down the curve of her cheek.

'I've spent a lot of time thinking about you, Genevieve,' he said softly. 'An awful lot of time just trying to convince myself that you couldn't possibly be as lovely and sweet as you appear.'

'Oh.' She swallowed hard, trying to ease the knot of tension and find some smart, sophisticated rejoinder to that startling revelation, but she couldn't. 'And did you succeed?'

He took her hand, linking his fingers with hers as he drew it on to the hard warm muscles of his thigh. 'I thought I had until I found your van last night. It brought home to me just how much you've come to mean to me these past few weeks.'

'Oh, Ross!' Turning to him, Genevieve tried to find the words to tell him how she felt, to explain all the new emotions blossoming inside her, but he laid a finger gently over her lips to stop her, a hint of sadness on his face.

'No, please don't say anything, Genevieve. There can be nothing between us. Deep down we both know that. That's why you stopped me from kissing you in the garden before. It was the right thing to do, the only sensible thing, because there's nothing I can offer you apart from an affair, and you wouldn't be happy with that, would you? I won't take a chance on losing the company.'

For a moment his hand tightened painfully round hers before he slowly let it go and started the engine, turning the car back on to the narrow track.

Genevieve sat back in her seat as she stared out of the window, feeling the hot sting of tears prick at her lowered lids. He was right, of course. There could be nothing between them, no sort of commitment, nothing but this strange all-consuming attraction. She couldn't allow herself to fall in love with him because in a contest between her and the company there could only ever be one winner. It was a bitter thought.

Moonlight filtered through the window, laying silvery fingers across her closed lids, and Genevieve stirred restlessly in the bed. She rolled over, burrowing her head into the pillow to block out the disturbing gleam of light, but it was far too hot to stay like that for long. Tossing the sheet aside, she climbed wearily out of the bed and walked to the window, pushing the tumbling mass of hair from her hot, flushed cheeks.

Below her, the garden lay still, all daytime colour drained by the silvery touch of the bright moonlight, like a photographic negative. In the distance she could hear the soft rustle of leaves as a tiny warm breeze stirred the trees, but apart from that everywhere was incredibly quiet. Nothing moved, nothing disturbed the pewter-dark shadows dappling the lawns or broke the sleeping house's silence. It seemed she was the only living thing awake that night.

With a sigh she turned away, her eyes touching on the rumpled bed without enthusiasm before sliding to the small clock on the bedside table. Three a.m. The most lonely time in the whole twenty-four hours when one was awake and alone. It was the time when a person started to look deep inside him or herself, to examine emotions and feelings which could be hidden during the busy bustle of the day. If she stood here much longer, awake and alone, then she would never be able to stop herself from thinking back over what had happened in that tiny secret clearing in the wood, would never be able to stop remembering Ross's face and what he'd said; and she didn't want to do that, didn't want to face the pain and heartache which would follow. All day and all night long since they'd got back she had played her part, pinning on a happy smile, laughing, talking, making merry for the benefit of Henry and the rest of her audience, but now she knew she couldn't pretend any longer. There were no more masks left in her cupboard, no more veils to hide behind, just she and the cold harsh truth in the quiet lonely silence of the night. The realisation terrified her.

She didn't want to stand here, alone, dwelling on what might have been, what could have happened between her and Ross if things had been different. She couldn't cope with that sort of pain. She had to find something to take her mind off it all, something to help the drugging pull of sleep return again, and though she doubted she could find anything as exotic as mandragora, which helped keep Cleopatra's mind off her Mark Antony, there must surely be something more prosaic. Perhaps a book would while away the hours and numb her mind enough to sleep again.

Pulling on the dainty cotton robe that matched her white broderie anglaise nightdress, Genevieve crept from the room and down the stairs, wincing every time a tread creaked noisily under her bare feet. Henry's house was old, the stairs uneven, and every single step she took sounded like the progress of an invading army. At this rate she would soon have the whole of the house awake and downstairs with her!

Finally she reached the bottom of the stairs and hurried across the hall, halting uncertainly outside the library door. Her mouth was parched, her throat dry with a combination of heat and tension, and suddenly the thought of a cooling glass of milk was too tempting to resist. Swinging round, she hurried along the hall and into the kitchen, using the dim light shining from the open fridge door to pour the drink by rather than switch on the light and risk waking anyone. She took a sip, savouring the cool clean taste as it slid down her throat.

'What's the matter? Can't you sleep either, Genevieve?'

The soft question was so unexpected that Genevieve swung round, the glass falling from her nerveless fingers to shatter on the hard tiled floor. Milk spattered the front of her gown, rained coldly on her bare feet, yet she never felt it as she stared with widened eyes at the tall figure standing by the door.

'Ross! You. . .oh, you did give me a fright! I

never heard you.' Instinctively she went to step forward, stopping abruptly as he called out an urgent warning.

'Stop! Stay there. You'll cut your feet if you step on any of that glass.'

In two long strides he crossed the kitchen, swinging her up in his arms as easily as if she were a child rather than a grown woman, and set her down gently by the kitchen door. For a moment his gaze lingered on her stunned face, a tiny gleam of fire in the blue depths of his eyes which made her breath catch tight in her chest, before he said quietly, 'Stay there while I clear it up.'

Finding a brush and pan in one of the cupboards, he set to work, wrapping the glittering, vicious splinters of glass into a thick newspaper before dropping them safely into the waste-bin. Still stunned by his unexpected appearance, Genevieve could only stand and watch him, her eyes lingering on the smooth flexing of hard muscles, the golden gleam of tanned skin. He was wearing only pyjama bottoms, the dark, silky material riding low on his lean hips, his torso bare, and he looked so devastatingly masculine that Genevieve felt her heart start to hammer wildly. Deep down, she knew she should really smile sweetly, thank him nicely, then hurry back to her room as fast as her legs could carry her, but somehow she just couldn't move a muscle. The night was hot, the air still, yet filled with such a sudden overpowering tension that she stayed rigid, caught in its hold like a butterfly in a net. For the life of her she couldn't walk away and leave him once again!

'There, that should do it, and no one should be any the wiser. Are you sure you're all right, though? You look rather pale. You haven't cut your feet, have you?'

Ross stood in front of her, his eyes moving down to her bare feet peeping from under the hem of the long gown before sliding back to her face and halting. Genevieve shook her head, too tense to speak, a tiny pulse beating frantically at the base of her throat as she looked back at him. For a moment there was silence, a heavy aching silence which seemed to hum with a thousand unspoken words and feelings, then slowly, slowly Ross bent and whispered, 'Genevieve,' just an instant before his mouth touched hers.

The kiss was soft, gentle, tender at first, then filled with a mounting heat and passion as she responded blindly, caught up in the sheer magic of the moment. With a low murmur, he pulled her to him, holding her so tightly against his chest that she could feel the heavy pounding of his heart against her breast. She moved closer, pressing her softness against his hardness, and heard him catch his breath in a sudden helpless gasp of longing. For a second he went rigid, his hands tightening round her shoulders as he drew back to stare deep into her eyes.

'This is wrong, Genevieve,' he ground out, his voice a hoarse whisper. 'Stop me, please, because lord knows I haven't got the strength to stop myself right now!'

For a second a tiny voice of reason filtered through the wild hot longing surging inside her, a cold little flicker of common sense, but it couldn't withstand the heat of passion firing her blood. She could have nothing of this man, nothing except this one glorious night: one night to make up for all the lonely ones which were to come. Common sense couldn't stand up against that temptation.

She looked up, her eyes filled with a soft invitation as she stared into his strained face. 'But I don't want to stop you, Ross. I don't want to fight against it any more.'

'Genevieve! No. . .we've got to be sensible,' he whispered urgently, his body trembling against hers.

'Do we?' she asked, smiling slowly, her hands sliding up the firm warm muscles to link round his neck. 'Do you really want to be sensible, Ross, right now?'

The words were a challenge and Ross reacted to them immediately. Pulling her back into his arms, he held her close, his lips trailing a frantic flurry of kisses up her cheek, tiny pinpoints of hot sensation which made her shudder and cling weakly to him.

'No, dammit! No, I don't want to be sensible any more, my love.'

'Then what do you want?' she asked, her lips brushing the faintly rough skin of his jaw. 'Tell me, Ross.'

'You! Just you, Genevieve!' And swung her up into his arms and carried her up the stairs and into his room.

CHAPTER TEN

THE heady fragrant smell of honeysuckle and old-
fashioned roses drifted in through the open window,
and Genevieve awoke. For a long, glorious moment
she lay quite still, a faint smile curving her lips as
she remembered the hours she and Ross had spent
together, the beauty and the magic of them. Happi-
ness welled up inside her and she stretched out her
hand, wanting to touch him, to feel the warm
smoothness of his skin again, the firm hardness of
his body, but the bed was empty. Ross had gone.

Clutching the sheet to her, Genevieve sat up,
staring round the room in sudden panic. Where was
he? Why had he just upped and left her without a
word, a kiss, or a tender gesture after all they had
shared? Had it really meant so little to him that he
could just walk out and leave her like that?

A cold *frisson* raced down her spine and she
climbed out of the bed, dragging the crumpled gown
over her head, somehow ashamed of her own nakedness and what it meant. Her heart was hammering,
a light, fast nervous tapping which made her feel
panicky and sick, and she swallowed hard to stem
the rising bile of fear. Picking up her robe, she
slipped it on and opened the bedroom door, her face
flaming as she came face to face with Henry in the
corridor. For a second he stared at her, his eyes
filled with fury as they slid past her to the rumpled

bed, before he took up his role of genial host once
again.

'Ah, Genevieve, good morning. I hope you slept
well? We've had breakfast, but there's toast and
coffee in the dining-room when you're ready. Don't
hurry.'

Genevieve went scarlet and looked away, wishing
the ground would open up and swallow her. Everything she and Ross had shared, every tender caress,
every magical touch, seemed somehow sullied,
soiled by this man and what he represented. She
hurried past him back to her own room and closed
the door, leaning against it as her legs threatened to
buckle. Closing her eyes, she attempted to get a grip
on herself, to fight against the rising debilitating
panic, but that was a mistake. Against the darkness
of her closed lids images appeared, fleeting, tormenting pictures of her and Ross, twined together,
making love with a wild abandon.

A moan broke from her lips and she pressed a
hand to her mouth, terrified that if she let it build
and grow she would never be able to stop it again.
Why had she done it? Why had she compromised all
her principles like that for a few hours of madness?
A few hours which would haunt her forever.

There was a low tapping at her door and she
jumped, her face pale as she turned to face it.

'Genevieve. . .can I come in? We need to talk.'

She couldn't face him, not now while her feelings
were still so raw. She needed time to get things back
into perspective.

'I—I'm not dressed yet. Can't it wait till later?'

'No, dammit, it can't. I know what you're think-ing, Genevieve. I know how you must be tormenting yourself about what happened last night.'

'Do you? Well, you should have thought of that before you walked out on me this morning!' Her voice broke and she turned away, feeling sick.

There was a low angry mutter, then the door opened abruptly and Ross walked into the room, his face grim as he saw her stricken expression. He walked over to the window, pushing his hands deep into the pockets of his linen trousers as he looked out, as though frightened he might reach out and touch her if he didn't. Genevieve watched him, drinking in the familiar lines and contours of his body which she knew now almost as intimately as her own, and shuddered with a wave of remembered passion. Turning away, she sat down at the dressing-table and pulled a brush through her tangled hair, brushing and brushing the silken length as though her life depended on it.

'I want to apologise for last night,' Ross said quietly. 'It should never have happened. It was a mistake.'

A mistake! All those magical hours summed up as an error of judgement? Genevieve felt her heart break at the thought that he could dismiss it all so easily. She drew the brush through her hair again, counting the strokes with a concentration that bor-dered on hysteria. Somehow she had to cope with this and not let him see just how his cruel words had hurt her.

'Genevieve, are you listening to me?'

Ross glanced sideways at her, his face tightening

as he saw her pallor, the way her hands trembled. He came closer, taking the brush from her hand before tilting her chin with a gentle finger so that she was forced to meet his eyes.

'We can't change what happened, Genevieve, can't make it go away by pretending. This morning when I woke up and the full implications of what we'd done hit me I. . .well, I really can't tell you how bad I felt. You trusted me, Genevieve. You agreed to help me and trusted me, and I betrayed that trust. Nothing can ever make up for that!

There was a tormented note in his deep voice, and Genevieve knew she couldn't let him torture himself like this, shoulder all the blame.

'No one *made* me sleep with you, Ross,' she said softly, her voice a bare whisper. 'I wanted to. You gave me a chance to say no and I refused it. I don't blame you for what happened, I suppose I don't really even blame myself. I think it was unavoidable, in the circumstances. If I was short with you just now it was because I was upset, waking like that, alone. It made it all seem so sordid somehow.'

'I had to, sweetheart, don't you see? If I'd stayed then the temptation would have been too great. I would have made love to you again this morning if I hadn't got up and left that room!'

'Oh.' There was little else she could find to say in the face of what was so obviously the truth. She looked down, staring at her hands which were nervously twisting the delicate cotton fabric of her robe. 'What are we going to do, Ross?'

He straightened, walking away to sit down on the end of the bed. 'I don't know. I really don't know where to go from here. I just wish I'd never started any of this, that I'd let events take their course and faced up to any possible takeover bid if and when it happened.'

'You only did what you thought was right; what you could to keep control of the company. Actually, I don't think you'll have much trouble with Henry for a while. He saw me coming out of your room and I think he had a pretty good idea of what had gone on.' Her face flushed, and Ross swore softly as he saw her embarrassment.

'What can I say, Genevieve, except that I'm sorry for putting you through all this? It seemed such a good idea at the beginning. I knew that if Henry and his cronies got an inkling of the truth about the bequest I would have a fight on my hands, and I just wasn't in a position to win. I *needed* this bit of breathing space our supposed alliance gave me. I just never realised what sort of effect it could have on both of us. Will you ever forgive me?'

Genevieve smiled shakily. 'You know I will. It wasn't your fault. There was no way you could guess that we might be attracted to each other.'

'No,' he agreed softly, his eyes steady on her face, 'I couldn't foresee that, but now it's happened, what are we going to do about it?'

'What can we do? I don't think we have that many options, Ross. I won't have an affair with you, if that's what you're suggesting.'

'I didn't think you would. So where do we go from here?'

Where do we go? A simple question, yet the answer was intolerably complex. They couldn't go back, return to their previous arrangement with the memory of last night lying between them, and they couldn't go forward, make any sort of commitment to each other.

Genevieve stood up and walked to the window, resting her forehead against the smooth, cold glass. Ross hadn't said he loved her and she didn't even know if she loved him. All they shared was this deep physical attraction, a fire in their blood. Even without the problem of the shares it was no basis for any sort of long-term commitment. . .no basis for marriage. The trouble was she was just so confused by what had happened that it was hard to think straight at the moment and come up with some sort of an answer.

'Well, Genevieve?' Ross prompted gently.

She stared out of the window, knowing her whole future could rest on her answer. Below her life was going on as normal, unaffected by the tension in this room. Philippe and Henry were sitting on the terrace, engrossed in an animated conversation. She could hear the soft rumble of their voices, the almost musical cadences of Philippe's accented tones, and suddenly a wave of loneliness swept over her, an overwhelming desire to run home to her mother and have her soothe away the hurt as she'd done so many times when Genevieve had been a child. Suddenly, in that split second, she knew exactly what she would do. She turned back to Ross, a new resolve in her face.

'I think it would be better if I went away for a while—a short holiday. No one will think it strange, not even Henry. I'm almost certain that he's convinced about our relationship now, so I doubt if you'll have any trouble from him, at least for a couple of weeks. Will that give you enough time to sort things out?'

Ross nodded, his face strangely bleak. 'Yes, it should do. I've made better headway than I hoped in building up my stock and another couple of weeks should see it through. But where will you go?' He stood up, moving closer to take her hands and hold them gently, his thumbs brushing lightly over their backs in a soft caress that made her blood race and her heart ache. 'I hate to think of you being alone, especially right now.'

Genevieve forced a smile to her lips and a brightness to her voice she was far from feeling. 'Oh, there's no danger of that! I'll go over to France and stay with my mother for a couple of weeks. I've been promising to go for ages now. There's no chance I'll be lonely there, with her around.'

'When will you go?'

'Probably the end of the week. I'll need to make a few arrangements for the shop first, though I doubt if there'll be a problem. Don't worry, Ross, I'll be fine.' She pulled away, knowing she couldn't bear to stay so close to him a moment longer. 'Now, if you'll excuse me, I'd better go and get dressed for the last act. I really think that today I'll give Henry a performance he'll remember!'

With a smile she hurried towards the adjoining bathroom, stopping abruptly as Ross spoke again.

'You told me once that you would only ever sleep

with a man if you loved him. Is that true,
Genevieve?'

Pain knifed through her, tearing into her heart so
fiercely that she almost staggered under the force of
it. She gripped hold of the doorframe, fighting
against the agony of it, fighting to keep any trace of
it from her voice.

'I don't think you have the right to ask me that,
Ross, nor the right to expect an answer, do you?'

Her hand slid to her side as she walked into the
bathroom and slowly closed the door.

In the end Genevieve never made it to France.
When she phoned her mother it was to find that
Madame Gray had already made arrangements to
spend some time with some friends. Although she
immediately offered to cancel her plans, Genevieve
wouldn't let her. Her mother was only now starting
to make a life for herself, three years after the death
of Genevieve's father, and there was no way that
Genevieve wanted to get in the way of it happening.

She could have arranged another holiday, she
supposed, booked into a hotel or picked up one of
the ever-abundant package deals, yet she didn't want
to do that. As Ross had so rightly guessed, she didn't
want to be alone right now, to have all those lonely
hours to think. She had to keep busy, fill her mind
and her days; it was the only way that she could
cope.

She went straight in to work on the Monday
morning and immersed herself in the business, getting up ridiculously early to buy the best blooms at
the flower market and keeping the shop open even

later than usual. It was a gruelling régime which left her body exhausted after a few days, yet her mind was still painfully active, still filled with haunting memories she didn't want to face. When Cathy rang in sick towards the end of the week, she welcomed the fact that she would be even busier than ever. Every time she let her mind wander she could hear Ross's voice again, asking that same disturbing question about why she'd slept with him, and she didn't want to face up to the truth of the answer. It was more than she could bear to do that.

Up to her eyes in a backlog of invoices and VAT forms one day when she was supposed to be having her lunch-break, she automatically answered the telephone when it rang, her mind still on the long columns of figures.

'Hearts & Flowers.'

There was a strange little pause and Genevieve repeated the greeting. 'Hearts & Flowers. Can I help you?'

'Gen? Is that really you?'

'Of course it is, Vicky. I do own the shop, remember?' Amused at the shock in her friend's voice, Genevieve smiled and set the pencil aside, glad of a diversion from the irritating columns, the pluses and minuses which wouldn't balance.

'Why, yes. . .yes, of course. It's just that Mr Harper said you were away. I must have got it wrong, I guess.'

There was a nervous note in Vicky's voice, a touch of unease which Genevieve found surprising. Why on earth should the girl feel nervous about speaking to her? She'd done it a hundred times before when she'd rung to chat. . .or place an order!

A cold wave of faintness swept over her as she suddenly realised what was wrong with Vicky. She had rung to place an order. . .flowers for Ross's latest girlfriend! Pain knifed through her and she closed her eyes as the whole room started to spin in sickening circles. As though from a great distance she could hear Vicky calling her name, yet it seemed to take forever before she could summon up the strength to answer.

'I'm still here, Vicky.'

'Are you all right? Look, maybe it would be better if I rang you later when. . .'

'No.' Abruptly Genevieve cut her off, shaking her head to clear the lingering mists of faintness before picking up the pencil and opening her pad with a steely determination. 'I take it you wanted to place an order, so why don't you give me the details?'

'Oh, Gen, I would never have rung if I'd realised you'd be in the shop.'

'Why not? After all, it's business, isn't it, Vicky, and that's all I'm interested in—business.'

'But you and Mr Harper——'

'I'll explain all that to you one day,' said Genevieve, a note of brittle amusement in her voice. 'I'm sure you'll enjoy hearing a good tale. Now if you'll just give me all the details.'

She took down the order, her hand shaking so much that the pencil curled and skipped across the paper so that the words were almost indecipherable, yet she knew that she would be able to read them. Every letter of the name and address was imprinted on her heart, mute testimony of just how little she really meant to Ross Harper.

'Right, thanks, Vicky. I've got all that. They'll be delivered this afternoon. OK?'

'Yes, that's fine, Gen. Look, I'm really sorry about this. I feel awful, really awful.'

'Don't. I'm grateful to you, Vicky.'

'Grateful? I don't understand.'

'Probably not, but let's just say that you've made me come to my senses at last.'

After murmuring goodbye, Genevieve replaced the receiver and sat still staring down at the order pad. Stephanie Beaumont, a lovely name for a lovely woman, if she knew anything at all about Ross. For a long moment she closed her eyes, desperately trying to conjure up an image of the woman, to put a face to the person who had suddenly shattered every single one of her dreams, but she couldn't. All she could picture was Ross, his eyes dark, his face tender, staring down at her in that instant before he had made her his.

Tears sprang to her eyes, hot, bitter tears, but impatiently she brushed them away. She wouldn't cry, wouldn't give in to this aching sense of loss which threatened to destroy her. All along Ross had told her that their arrangement was purely business. She couldn't blame him; it had been her own blind stupidity which had tried to turn it into something more, something it could never be. Ross had taken her to bed last week because she'd been there, willing and available. There was no way she could continue to delude herself that it had meant more to him that that. She had to face up to the truth, deliver the flowers and see for herself the kind of woman Ross Harper *really* wanted in his life.

With a leaden heart Genevieve arranged the flowers, then locked the shop and drove across town to the address Vicky had given her. There were double yellow lines painted all along the road, but she ignored them, parking the van slap bang in front of the tall elegant Victorian house. Picking up the flowers from the passenger seat, she walked slowly up the path and rang the bell, closing her eyes as another sudden wave of giddiness assailed her. She fought it down, breathing slowly and deeply as she clung on to what little remained of her composure, yet nothing could have prepared her for the shock when the door swung open. For a full horror-filled minute Genevieve stared up at the tall man framed in the doorway, her eyes drinking in the sight of him while every single cell in her body screamed out a denial. He couldn't be here, he just couldn't! It seemed too cruel a blow on top of the ones she'd already sustained that day.

'Genevieve!' Shock echoed through his deep voice, etched lines of strain on his handsome face. 'Genevieve. . .I don't believe this! What on earth are you doing here?'

'I. . .' Glancing down at the bouquet crushed in her arms, Genevieve tried to find some way to answer. 'The flowers you ordered.' She held them out to him, but he ignored them, his eyes fastening on the pallor of her face, the faint tremble that assailed her body.

'Are you all right, sweetheart? You look rather shaken. Come inside and let me get you a drink.'

Stepping out on to the path, he attempted to lead her into the house, but Genevieve hung back, knowing she couldn't cope with the sight of him and the other woman together.

'No, I don't want to come in—I'm all right. Let me go!' Her voice was shrill, tinged with a rising hysteria, and Ross shot her a startled look.

'Don't be silly, Genevieve! Of course you're not all right. You're shaking.' He ran his hands gently down her arms, his touch light yet leaving behind it a lingering echo of sensation which Genevieve reacted violently to.

'Take your hands off me, Ross Harper! I don't want you to touch me. . .ever!'

'Since when?' he demanded, advancing a step towards her. 'Since when has my touch been so repellent to you? I don't remember you shying away from me last weekend.'

How could he? How could he torture her like that, throwing the memories back at her? With a tiny sob Genevieve thrust the flowers at him, uncaring that several of the fragile stems snapped under such rough treatment, then took to her heels and fled down the path and climbed into the van. She was shaking, her whole body trembling so hard that she couldn't seem to fit the key into the ignition. Tears of frustration and pain clouded her eyes and she brushed them away as she tried again, desperate to get as far away from this house and that man as she could. Suddenly the passenger door swung open and Ross climbed in beside her, his face filled with a mounting fury. Yet what right did he have to glare at her like that? She was the injured party.

'Get out!' she shouted, the very last of her control snapping. 'Get out of my van right now, Ross Harper!' With a little click the key slid into place and she started the engine with a mighty roar.

'No chance. I'm staying right here till you tell me what's wrong,' he said quietly, though there was nothing quiet about the expression on his face.

'Well, you're going to have a long wait, because I've no intention of telling you anything! Now get out, get out before I. . .I. . .' Her mind went blank. For the life of her she couldn't think of a single thing to threaten him with.

'Till you what, Genevieve?' he queried softly, reaching out to switch off the engine and take the key from her nerveless fingers. 'Till you hit me over the head again like you did last time? I almost wish you would, you know. Maybe it would knock some sense back into me and stop all these crazy thoughts that keep filling my head.'

There was no anger in his deep voice now, just a wry trace of humour—and something else, something which made her feel breathless.

'What do you mean?'

He smiled slowly, watching her face as he said softly, 'Simply that I've not been the same man since that first meeting. All I seem to be able to think about recently is you, Genevieve, or you and me, together in that bed. Do you remember what it was like, the two of us so close, bodies touching, meeting in the quiet stillness of that night?'

Did she remember? How could she forget? How could she resist the sweet seductive spell his words were creating?

'Yes,' she whispered. 'Yes, Ross, but——'

He leant forward, pressing a finger gently against her parted lips. 'No "buts", Genevieve. There can be no "buts" in love, and that's what it was that night—love. Nothing less. You wouldn't have slept with me without love.'

He was right, of course. Deep down she had known it all along but had been terrified to face it, terrified to answer the question he had asked her. She loved him, loved him with all her heart and soul, and that was the only reason she had spent that night in his arms. She nodded, not yet able to put her feelings into words.

'Thank God! Oh, thank God I was right, Genevieve!' He pulled her to him, holding her close so that she could feel the heavy shudders that shook his body. 'I've been so afraid I was wrong, darling. So afraid that you'd been caught up in the magic of the moment and that it wasn't love you'd felt for me. I've been going crazy this past week, not able to talk to you, thinking you were away. I was terrified that you would convinvce yourself that you couldn't possibly be in love with me, and I couldn't have borne that. I love you, Genevieve, you see.'

'Ross!' Stunned by the confession, Genevieve pulled back, her eyes huge, colour ebbing and flowing in her cheeks. 'You can't mean that!'

'Can't I? Let me show you.'

Fire licked along her veins as his lips closed over hers, fanning into a great blaze as his hands moulded her against him. With a tiny moan Genevieve wrapped her arms round his neck, kissing him back with all the pent-up longing she'd held in check this past long week. He loved her! Just the thought made her heart race and her body burn with longing. No matter what happened no one could take that from her.

Finally, when they were both spent and breathless, Ross drew back, running his hand gently down the side of her face. Turning her head, Genevieve nipped his palm, smiling as she heard the strained gasp which he couldn't quite hide.

'Genevieve! Don't do that, not unless you want Great-Aunt Stephanie and all her neighbours to be shocked rigid.'

'Great-Aunt Stephanie? You mean those flowers were for your aunt!' She glanced towards the crumpled cellophane package lying lonely and abandoned on the path.

'Of course. It's her birthday today; she's eighty.' Ross laughed when he saw her expression, his eyes dancing at her obvious embarrassment. 'Did you think they were for a girlfriend, Genevieve? Come on, confess!'

'Well, how was I to know that she's your aunt?' Blushing hotly, Genevieve tried to wriggle free, but Ross wouldn't let her go, planting a hard kiss on her lips that left her reeling.

'That's for doubting me so readily, Genevieve Gray, and if you're not careful there'll be more of that sort of punishment!'

'Yes, please,' she replied, brazenly moving closer, loving the way his body reacted immediately to her closeness.

'If there wasn't a traffic warden heading this way,

all ready to book you for illegal parking on double yellow lines, I would take you up on that, lady.'

'What! Oh, quick,Ross, give me the keys. I hate paying parking fines.' Spotting the man heading in their direction, Genevieve held her hand out for the van keys.

'In a minute, when you've agreed to something.'

'Agreed to what? Oh, please, Ross, can't it wait! Give me the keys!'

'Will you marry me?'

For a full minute Genevieve forgot all about the approaching warden as she stared at Ross, her eyes huge and startled. She licked her suddenly dry lips and said slowly, 'Did I hear you right? Did you ask me to marry you?'

'Yes.'

'But how can I? What about the shares? Is this some sort of a joke?'

'It's no joke, Genevieve. I love you. I want you to marry me, so what's your answer?'

'But we can't, Ross. You might lose the company; you can't risk it!'

'The company doesn't mean a thing to me, not if it means I can't have you. I realised that last weekend, after you'd left, realised that I had to finally stop trying to fool myself that all I felt for you was some sort of physical attraction. It's more than that, so much more that it terrifies me. I've spent years, you see, trying to avoid any sort of commitment, yet along you come and all of a sudden my life is turned upside down. I love you, Genevieve, and I want to marry you, want to know that you're mine completely. I can face anything that happens with the company as long as I have you by my side. So come on, sweetheart, make your choice: a parking ticket or a marriage licence. It's a fair trade, isn't it?'

He dangled the keys temptingly on the end of his finger, his eyes sparkling with laughter and so much love that Genevieve felt her knees turn to water. A fair trade, he'd called it. Well, as far as she could see it was the best deal she'd ever been offered! How could she refuse when it was what she wanted so desperately?

Leaning over, she kissed him hard on the lips. 'Yes. Yes, I'll marry you, Ross Harper. Now give me those keys before we both end up in court!'

Snatching them from him, she started the engine and pulled away from the kerb, blowing a kiss at the startled traffic warden as she roared joyfully past him.

Dust motes danced in the air, tickling her nose, and Genevieve searched in her bag for a handkerchief to catch the impending sneeze. Across the room Ross was staring out of the window, tension showing in every rigid line of his body, and Genevieve's hand faltered as she saw it. Suddenly she knew she had to give him one last chance to change his mind, no matter how much the idea terrified her.

'If you decide you can't bear to go through with it, I'll understand, Ross, really I will. I know how much the company means to you, and it won't change how I feel about you if you can't bear to take a chance on losing it.'

He swung round, his face calm, his blue eyes steady as they met hers across the width of the room.

'The only thing I can't bear to lose is you, Genevieve. You're far more important to me than any company. I love you.'

Her heart raced frantically at the note in his deep voice and she glanced away, jumping slightly as the door suddenly opened and Mr Swan hurried into the room.

'Miss Gray. . .Mr Harper. What can I do for you?' There was a marked coolness about his greeting, which Genevieve could well appreciate after what had gone on the last time they'd been in his office together. However, surprisingly, the coolness soon changed to genuine pleasure when Ross explained the reason for their visit.

'Why, that's wonderful news, absolutely wonderful! Your grandfather would have been delighted. He left me a letter for you both just in case this very thing happened. I'll fetch it.'

He hurried out of the room, and Genevieve looked at Ross in total astonishment.

'What on earth did he mean about your grandfather, Ross? I thought he made the will to deliberately keep us apart!'

'Heaven knows, but I always had a feeling that there was more to the bequest than we were told about at first. I wonder what Grandfather was really up to. Still, who cares? As long as I have you that's all I'm bothered about.'

He kissed her hungrily on the lips so that she was flushed and breathless when Mr Swan hurried back into the room, coughing discreetly when he found them in each other's arms.

'Now I think this will explain everything, Mr

Harper. I'll leave you to read it. I rather think you're in for a surprise, both of you.' Smiling benignly, he handed a long pale cream envelope to Ross, then left the room. For a long minute Ross stared down at it, his face strangely tense.

'Open it, Ross. The suspense is killing me!'

Genevieve's anguished plea made him smile. He ripped the envelope open and drew out the letter, skimming down it with a mounting disbelief on his face.

'I don't believe it. . .I really don't believe it!' Suddenly he laughed, the sound echoing and rolling round the room, and Genevieve moved towards him, wondering if the shock had somehow unhinged him.

'What is it? What does it say? Ross!'

Wiping the tears of laughter from his eyes, Ross handed her the letter, watching the dawning comprehension on her face. She looked up at him, unable to believe what she'd read.

'But this means that the shares won't have to be sold after all, that it was all a trick; your grandfather's way of bringing us together yet ensuring that you couldn't marry me just to get them. I can't believe it!'

'Oh, I can, Genevieve. I can! The cunning old devil! He was always shrewd. He knew you were the right woman for me and knew that I'd run a million miles if he even hinted at it. The bequest was the perfect way of bringing us together and letting events run their course.'

'He always said I reminded him of your grandmother,' she said slowly, looking down at the letter, her eyes misted with tears.

Ross nodded, his face incredibly tender as he pulled her into his arms and held her close. 'He loved her very much, Genevieve, so it was the greatest compliment he could ever pay you. Theirs was the perfect marriage, just as ours will be.'

'Oh, Ross!' Lifting her face, she looked straight into his eyes. 'What can I say? Everything has turned out so much better than I ever dared hope it would.'

'Try "I love you, Ross",' he instructed, smiling down at her.

Genevieve laughed softly as she twined her arms round his neck and repeated obediently, 'I love you, Ross, I really do—but how did it happen? The last time we were here in this very office I was terrified that you were going to try and foreclose on the lease to my shop, while now——'

'Now the only lease I'm interested in is a permanent one, for your love. A lifetime's commitment, Genevieve, nothing less, but can you handle that sort of a contract?'

'Yes, Ross, yes, yes and yes again!'

Drawing his head down, she kissed him, sealing the contract in a very effective way indeed!

 **Mills & Boon**

4 ROMANCES & 2 GIFTS - YOURS ABSOLUTELY FREE!

An irresistible invitation from Mills & Boon! Please accept our offer of 4 free books, a pair of decorative glass oyster dishes and a special MYSTERY GIFT...Then, if you choose, go on to enjoy 6 more exciting Romances every month for just £1.35 each postage and packing free.

**Send the coupon below at once to -
Reader Service, FREEPOST, P.O. Box 236, Croydon, Surrey CR9 9EL**

✂ - *No stamp required* -

YES! Please rush me my **4 Free Romances and 2 FREE Gifts !** Please also reserve me a Reader Service Subscription. so I can look forward to receiving 6 Brand New Romances each month, for just £8.10 total. Post and packing is **free**, and there's a free monthly Mills & Boon Newsletter. If I choose not to subscribe I shall write to you within 10 days - I understand I can keep the books and gifts whatever I decide. I can cancel or suspend my subscription at any time, I am over18.

EP60R

NAME _____

ADDRESS _____

_____

_____ *POSTCODE* _____

SIGNATURE _____

 mps MAILING PREFERENCE SERVICE

TWO COMPELLING READS FOR MAY 1990

TESS *Katherine Burton* £2.99

In the third book of this sensational quartet of sisters, the bestselling author of *Sweet Summer Heat* creates Tess. Tormented by the guilt of her broken marriage and afraid to risk the pain again, Tess is torn by desire. But was Seth Taylor the right choice in helping her to get over the pain of the past?

SPRING THUNDER *Sandra James* £2.99

After a traumatic divorce and the unfamiliar demands of a new born son, Jessica is determined to start a new life running a garden centre. Tough, reliable Brody was hired to help, but behind the facade of job hunting is hidden the fact that he was being paid to destroy Jessica…whatever the cost.

W**O**RLDWIDE

Just answer these simple questions for your FREE book

1. Who is your favourite author? _____

2. The last romance you read *(apart from this one)* was? _____

3. How many Mills & Boon Romances have you bought in the last 6 months? _____

4. How did you first hear about Mills & Boon? *(Tick one)*
   - ☐ Friend ☐ Television ☐ Magazines or newspapers
   - ☐ Saw them in the shops ☐ Received a mailing
   - ☐ other *(please describe)* _____

5. Where did you get this book?

   _____

6. Which age group are you in?
   - ☐ Under 24 ☐ 25-34 ☐ 35-44
   - ☐ 45-54 ☐ 55-64 ☐ Over 65

7. After you read your Mills & Boon novels, what do you do with them?
   - ☐ Keep them ☐ Give them away
   - ☐ Lend them to friends
   - ☐ Other *(Please describe)*

   _____
   _____

8. What do you like about Mills & Boon Romances?

   _____

9. Are you a Mills & Boon subscriber? ☐ Yes ☐ No

Fill in your name and address, put this page in an envelope and post TODAY to: **Mills & Boon Reader Survey, FREEPOST, P.O. Box 236, Croydon, Surrey. CR9 9EL**

NO STAMP NEEDED

Name (Mrs. / Miss. / Ms. / Mr.) _____

Address _____
_____

_____ Postcode _____

You may be mailed with offers as a result of this questionnaire

PWQ1

2 NEW TITLES FOR JUNE 1990

PASSAGES by Debbi Bedford
Shannon Eberle's dreams had catapulted her to the height of fame and fortune in New York City. But when the lights went out on Broadway, she found herself longing for home and the people she'd left behind. So Shannon returned to Wyoming, where she met Peter Barrett, a strong and gentle man who taught her to dream anew...
£2.99

ALL MY TOMORROWS by Karen Young
Carly Sullivan was a woman who trusted her heart. For her it was easy to see the solution to the problems Jess Brannigan was having with his estranged son. For Jess, seeing what a little tender loving care could achieve was a revelation. An even greater surprise was the difference Carly made in his own life!
£2.99

WORLDWIDE

DREAM SONG TITLES COMPETITION
HOW TO ENTER

Listed below are 5 incomplete song titles. To enter simply choose the missing word from the selection of words listed and write it on the dotted line provided to complete each song title.

A. . . . . .DREAMS   LOVER

B.   DAY DREAM . . . .   ELECTRIC

C.   DREAM . . . .   CHRISTMAS

D.   . . . . UPON A DREAM   BELIEVER

E.   I'M DREAMING OF A WHITE . . . .   ONCE

When you have completed each of the song titles, fill in the box below, placing the songs in an order ranging from the one you think is the most romantic, through to the one you think is the least romantic.

Use the letter corresponding to the song titles when filling in the five boxes. For example: If you think C. is the most romantic song, place the letter C. in the 1st box.

	1st	2nd	3rd	4th	5th
LETTER OF CHOSEN SONG					

MRS/MISS/MR . . . .

ADDRESS . . . .

. . . .

POSTCODE . . . . COUNTRY . . . .

CLOSING DATE: 31st DECEMBER, 1990
PLEASE SEND YOUR COMPLETED ENTRY TO EITHER:
Dream Book Offer, Eton House, 18-24 Paradise Road, Richmond, Surrey, ENGLAND TW9 1SR.
OR (Readers in Southern Africa)
Dream Book Offer, IBS Pty Ltd., Private Bag X3010, Randburg 2125, SOUTH AFRICA.

- -

Please retain this section.

RULES AND CONDITIONS
FOR THE COMPETITION AND DREAM BOOK OFFER